# HUSHED WORDS

Cassie, a struggling single mother, and Jay, a wealthy financier, share a holiday romance in Italy; when fate throws them together again their sizzling passion rekindles. Cassie's family problems combined with Jay's fear of commitment and growing dissatisfaction with his lifestyle make their idea of a future together a dream. Jay can't ask for a second chance with Cassie until he discovers a new direction in life and lays it all on the line with the woman he loves.

# ANGELA BRITNELL

# HUSHED WORDS

*Complete and Unabridged*

## LINFORD
*Leicester*

First published in Great Britain

First Linford Edition
published 2013

A catalogue record for this book is available
from the British Library.

ISBN 978–1–4448–1755–3

Published by
F. A. Thorpe (Publishing)
Anstey, Leicestershire

Set by Words & Graphics Ltd.
Anstey, Leicestershire
Printed and bound in Great Britain by
T. J. International Ltd., Padstow, Cornwall

This book is printed on acid-free paper

# 1

*If you wish to know the mind of a man, listen to his words.* — Chinese Proverb

Jay's gaze returned repeatedly to the cute blonde stretched out by the pool.

Tomorrow he'd head home to London but today was his reward. This vision in the red bikini, clinging temptingly in all the right places, lay there alone. She probably thought her sunglasses hid everything but the slight tilt of her head and the way her stomach muscles visibly tightened gave her away. She knew he was watching.

He stretched himself upright to standing, rolled his shoulders to unravel the kinks, and strolled over.

'Are you as bored as I am? I thought I'd come and say hello to the only other person around here under retirement

1

age. The name's Jay Burton.'

Long, slender fingers pushed the sunglasses up into her mass of shiny, blonde corkscrew curls. Her eyes, the darkest shade of blue he'd ever seen, fixed on him.

'Cassandra. Cassandra Moore. What are you doing here in the first place if it's so awful?'

'I'll tell you the story if you take pity on a lonely man. Why don't you have dinner with me by the lake and we'll watch the sun set together.'

Surely she wouldn't fall for such a clichéd line?

'Is it a long story?'

Her warm smile should've made him feel guilty but he sat down on the empty sun lounger next to her and she smiled right back, encouraging him to make his next move.

Jay picked up one of her warm hands, stroked a finger up to her wrist, rested it on her racing pulse, and murmured very, very slowly, 'I can make it last all night.'

They surely both knew he wasn't talking about the story.

She studied him again and gave a brief nod before allowing her sunglasses to fall back down and cover her enigmatic eyes.

* * *

Why the heck was he thinking of her tonight? They'd only shared one sultry, Italian summer night but he'd come close to truly connecting with a woman for the first time. Rubbish. He must be losing his mind.

Jay kicked off his glossy black Bruno Magli loafers, letting them lie where they fell beside the steel and glass coffee table. He draped the jacket of his silver gray Armani suit and the yellow Italian silk tie on the arm of the oversized black leather sofa. He opened the top buttons of his handmade white linen shirt and rolled up the sleeves, then, with a glass of Irish whiskey burning its way down his throat, Jay started to relax.

He flicked the switch to open the blinds and stepped out onto his balcony, determined to enjoy the stunning view out over Canary Wharf — after all he'd forked out over a million pounds out of his last bonus check for the privilege. He gazed across to Greenwich, his vision sweeping across the tall buildings of the financial center and over the fancy restaurants and shops along the river. This was where he belonged now and he'd keep telling himself that until he believed it.

He should go back in, fire up his laptop and do some research on the development company one of his clients was interested in, but his mind jangled with a mess of conflicting thoughts, none of which were very productive.

Annabelle expected him to call tonight but every boring conversation with her revolved around shopping, visits to the spa and the miniscule amount of work she'd done at the art gallery where she pretended to make a living. They'd dated for six whole weeks, which was at least five more than he would've liked, but somehow he had just let it drift.

Jay reluctantly went back inside and stretched out on the sofa. He aimed the TV remote and lay back to channel surf on his new indulgence — a fifty-inch plasma high-def digital set. He connected his laptop to the TV and scrolled through emails, deleting the junk, thankful he wasn't ready for Viagra yet.

Tony Raines . . . the name jumped out at him. Last time he'd heard his old friend was on a trek to Nepal to find himself or some such nonsense. Presumably he'd succeeded and was back in the land of relative normality.

Jay clicked open the message and his brow furrowed as he read through it a couple of times. Tony was now running a small bookshop in Cornwall specialising in Celtic works. The place was probably draped in crystals and frequented by long-haired weirdoes who thumbed through the books but couldn't afford to buy anything.

*Why don't you come and visit for a weekend and get away from the unhealthy air in London? Give me a call.*

Tony had plainly been reading too much Green Party literature. Jay moved the cursor over *Reply* ready to decline the offer, but hesitated. Easter was in a few weeks and the office would grind to a halt for several days. Annabelle kept dropping unsubtle hints about dragging him home to her family's Surrey mansion so this would make the perfect excuse.

Before he could think better of it Jay tapped the numbers into his mobile phone.

'Tony? Jay here.'

'Hey, stranger. How's it going?'

Tony's familiar voice eased something in him and Jay smiled.

'Not bad. Thought I might take you up on your offer, if you haven't changed your mind.'

'Great. When?'

'How about the Easter weekend, Friday until Monday?'

He'd dutifully gone home at Christmas and wasn't ready for another session of his family's favorite game show of Marry Jay Off. His mother was very unsubtle and the number of pretty, single girls who'd just happened to drop by the house was remarkable. To his family he'd always be the cute baby to be fussed over. With five older siblings he'd been the fun afterthought to a supposedly complete family. They were all married and the last time he counted Jay was uncle to fifteen.

'Sounds good. What're you up to these days?'

'Exactly what I told you I would. I made my first million by twenty-five and now I'm the youngest partner in the history of the firm with a corner office, a penthouse flat in Canary Wharf and the 2008 black BMW M6 convertible, fully loaded.'

A heavy silence hung between them

and Jay wished he'd kept his mouth shut.

'Are you happy?' was all Tony asked.

'Of course,' Jay snapped back and quickly ended the conversation, not wanting to drag up any more of the past.

Another dark mood seized him and his mind filled with midnight blue eyes, a wild mass of blonde curls, and a body that drove a man mad. Cassandra Moore would cure what ailed him tonight the same as she'd done last July in Lake Garda.

* * *

Cassie stepped out of the lift and Jay had sucked in a deep breath, stunned by the radiant smile she threw in his direction.

'Hey, you look wonderful.' Jay stepped across from the reception desk and his penetrating gaze roved over her, admiring the way her sapphire blue dress clung subtly to every feminine curve. 'We have a table booked on the terrace.'

He held out his arm and she hesitated, but only for a second.

They had talked for hours over dinner although he revealed little of his real life and he suspected she held back too, and he didn't question too deeply. As the sun set he took hold of her hand and stared deep into her smiling eyes.

'Would you care for a nightcap in my suite, Cassandra?'

She'd sucked in a quick breath and answered with the faintest tremble in her voice. 'Why not?'

Jay had ushered them upstairs and unlocked his door, gesturing for her to step inside. He kicked the door shut then gently took hold of her hands. 'No second thoughts?' She shook her head and he smiled. 'Good.'

His body tightened as he remembered their incredible lovemaking and how soft and warm she'd been in his arms the next morning. He needed to push her out of his head in record time or he'd go crazy.

He picked up his phone again and dialled.

'Hey, Annabelle, Jay. I just got home. You fancy a late dinner at First Edition before coming back here? I need you, darlin' girl.'

Annabelle fell for it in a second. All he ever had to do was turn up the Irish charm and she melted.

Dwelling on the past was a mugs' game.

\* \* \*

Cassie pushed Sam through the front door of their house, still shaking from the humiliating hour at the police station.

'Why, Sam? Why spray paint swear words on the church door? You're lucky the vicar isn't going to prosecute but you'll have to clean it off tomorrow — and do a good job or he might change his mind.'

With a sneer worthy of James Dean,

Sam rubbed a large hand over his shaved head and flexed his right arm, showing off the new barbed wire tattoo snaked around his bicep.

'Oh yeah, like you and some vicar's gonna make me.' His sharp, dark eyes dismissed her as he tossed a packet of cigarettes on the sofa, shaking one out ready to light.

Cassie snatched it from his fingers and threw it to the floor. 'You're not stupid, Sam, why do this?'

'Aw come on, Mum, stick to the script. It's supposed to be, you'll end up in prison like your no-good father if you carry on.'

Tiredness spread through every cell in her body. 'Go to bed, Sam, and stay there for once. We'll talk tomorrow.'

'I can hardly wait.' He slouched off up the stairs flipping open his mobile as he went.

She should take the phone away, ban him from going out, force him to go to school or get a job. Cassie held her throbbing head at the thought.

11

Sitting over her solitary breakfast Cassie read the Help Wanted ad for the tenth time, picked up the phone and set it back down again on the table. It was a waste of time because no book shop would want her. The fact that she read every book she could get her hands on wouldn't overcome the fact that she'd left school at sixteen and since then worked at just about anything to bring in money.

'Hello, Keltek Books, Tony Raines speaking.'

Cassie froze, not even realising she'd dialed the number.

She couldn't be rude. 'Hello. This is Cassie Moore. I saw your advert . . . ' Her voice trailed away.

'Oh, that's great. I'm desperate for help. Could you come in tomorrow for a chat?'

She'd dreaded the man would be a posh intellectual but he sounded normal enough. 'I'd like that. Would ten o'clock be OK?' She bit her tongue wondering if she should've waited for him to suggest a time.

'That's fine. My shop's on Lime Street, the narrow street you cut through to get to the cathedral.'

'I know where that is. I'll be there. Thanks.'

Her hands trembled as she hung up. For once she wanted a job for what it involved instead of only for the pay check at the end of the week.

What to wear was the next problem. Cassie didn't own any proper interview clothes. She mentally ran through her choices and decided the blue skirt she'd renovated from the charity shop plus a white scooped neck blouse she'd picked up at the market last week would have to do.

Lying in bed she tried to talk herself into sleep because Tony Raines wouldn't be impressed by the dark circles habitually under her eyes recently. She yawned and checked the clock. Midnight and Sam was still out, she'd heard him leave

13

earlier despite everything she'd said. Again. A year ago she'd have gone out searching for him. Nowadays if she said anything he laughed and told her he was sixteen and if she wasn't careful he'd leave home and join his traveler friends in Wales. If she dared to complain her parents said it was all her own fault; when you were a single parent there was no-one to share the blame.

She bet that Jay Burton sure as hell wasn't lying alone in his bed worrying about a troublesome teenage son.

Why on earth did he slip into her mind tonight after all these months? Believing that he'd call had been more than stupid — had she seriously thought a man on the last night of his holiday wanted anything other than a quick fling? She'd only been enjoying the expensive hotel as paid companion to a crabby old woman and spent her whole week fussing over Enid Williams, taking her on short trips around the area and making sure she had cardigans and scarves handy when it was drafty.

Her afternoon lounging by the pool and that magical night with Jay Burton was an unexpected gift when Enid suffered one of her migraines and wanted to be left alone.

Cassie knew she shouldn't indulge but it'd been a long, hard day so she allowed herself the luxury of stretching out in the lounger and remembering the man who'd awakened a side of her she hadn't known existed . . .

'No second thoughts?'

She shook her head and a devilish smile crept across his handsome face.

He molded his warm, firm lips to hers and Cassie tasted wine and potent desire on his tongue. She sank into him, moaning deep in the back of her throat. His hand eased around her back and slowly opened her zipper and then pushed the dress off her shoulders and down to the floor, gently holding her hand while she stepped out onto the thick, red carpet.

With gentle care he undid her bra and tossed it out of the way before his large hands circled her hips and in one swift move slid her black lace panties over her hips to the floor.

'I need you right now, OK?'

She nodded, not trusting herself to speak. As he stripped off Cassie flushed at the sight of his lean fit body, tanned to the color of golden syrup.

Jay swept her up into his arms, ignoring her gasp of surprise, and stepped across the room to lay her on the bed.

'You're so beautiful,' he said, his gaze roaming over every inch of her skin and she tingled with anticipation as his hands cupped her breasts. He stroked and teased until she writhed helplessly under him.

Suddenly Jay sat back; she moaned at the loss of his touch.

'Hang on, sweetheart.' He grabbed a foil packet from the bedside table and she flushed as she realised he'd had the foresight to take care of them both.

Jay shifted position and Cassie trembled, suddenly nervous. It had been so long for her and was never a great experience, she was afraid she might not be any good at this. Jay sensed her unease and cradled her face with his hands, stroking his large thumbs down her cheeks and kissing her without mercy until her body relaxed and opened to him.

Cassie exhaled a loud sigh as he pushed into her, holding himself still for a moment for her to adjust to the fullness of him before he began a slow, steady rhythm. She wrapped her legs around his waist and flexed her hips, urging him on. Nothing existed except him, the two of them, this moment. She was hanging on the edge but then Jay's hand snaked between them and his fingers pressed against the perfect spot to send her crashing into a spiral of pleasure. Vaguely Cassie was aware he'd reached his own release, pulsing deep inside her until neither of them had anything left to give.

Gently, he slid out of her and rolled back on to the bed, then wrapped her in his strong arms. Cassie dropped her head to his broad chest and silently, they both fell into a deep sleep.

Cassie flushed at how foolish she'd been the next morning, naively finding a piece of paper and giving him her name and phone number when he'd asked, probably out of courtesy.

Strangely enough it hadn't been because of his delicious lovemaking but rather the hint of vulnerability she'd seen his silvery blue eyes. He hadn't wanted her to see beneath his surface charm but she wasn't dumb. She'd left him with a bright smile and her fingers crossed and then routine life took over again and pushed him to the back of her mind — except for a few indulgent times like tonight.

With a sigh Cassie forced herself back to reality. Tomorrow she'd get the job, make enough money to get her own home and encourage Sam back into school.

Cassie finally drifted off to sleep, slipping back into her dream world with a new fantasy of being fed slices of overripe peaches by a gloriously naked Irishman. Crazy, but at least it would stop her from hearing when Sam eventually staggered home.

# 2

'Take this one home with you.' Tony pushed the book on ancient Celtic monuments into her hand. 'We need to know as much as possible about the books we sell in order to help the customers. You can give me the potted version when you've read it. Take your time.'

'Thanks.' Cassie tucked it into her bag and checked her watch. She said a quick goodbye and ran off down the street to the bus stop just as her bus pulled up. She jumped on and collapsed into the nearest spare seat.

She'd got through her first week as the new assistant at Keltek Books and loved every minute. Surrounded by books and working with such an easygoing man she wondered if maybe her luck was turning.

Sam mocked her when she told him about the job.

'It'll suit you to be stuck in some shop with a load of stupid old books. Bet the moron who owns it's a right one too. I mean what sort of real man does that for a job?'

She'd been surprised by her first sight of Tony so didn't blame Sam for jumping to conclusions. Not much older than her, tall and slim with laughing bright green eyes, Tony could definitely draw any woman's eyes. Every day as they shut the door at half past five he pulled the elastic band from his ponytail and shook out his thick, blond shoulder length hair.

He intrigued her but she wasn't about to dig any deeper. Cassie didn't need the extra aggravation men caused.

At the next stop Cassie dragged herself up and got off the bus, ready for another fun evening in the Moore household.

\* \* \*

'Is that you, dear?'

Who else did her mother think it was? Barbara Moore never encouraged the neighbors to walk in without being asked and, unsurprisingly, didn't have all that many friends, if any.

'Yes, Mum.'

Cassie hung up her old black raincoat in the dark hallway, dragging her heels before entering the stifling hot living room. Neither of her parents moved around much these days and they felt the cold more than she did.

'Hope you've got something decent for our tea tonight. Your father and I are fed up of sausages and baked beans. It's not good for our digestions.'

Cassie bit hard on her lip. They'd only had sausages once this week; no doubt the pasties she'd picked up on the way home would be another cause for complaint. They weren't a patch on homemade ones but it was six o'clock already and too late to start making anything. She could keep them until tomorrow and find something else.

'I'll go and see what's in the fridge.'

Her father snorted. 'That'll be a waste of bloody time. That scavenger you call a son has cleaned the place out. We had to make do with tinned soup for lunch.'

Cassie almost replied it was better than her miserly pot of yogurt but kept quiet. Her parents had taken care of her and Sam when she was desperate and this was payback time.

'I brought home some pasties, the good steak ones from the butchers, will that be all right?'

She took the muttered answers as agreement and retreated back to the kitchen. She soon had the table laid, the pasties on plates and a pot of tea made.

'Where's Sam?' She asked, then kicked herself.

Her father glared across the table. 'You're his mother. You should know. That Lindy Retallick came to the door earlier, smiling like butter wouldn't melt in her mouth and your wonderful son went off with her. I asked when he was coming back and he ignored me. Nice manners you've taught him.'

The food on her plate turned to sawdust and Cassie longed to rest her head on the table and weep.

They ate the rest of the meal in silence.

By the time she'd cleared up the kitchen, put some washing on to take advantage of the cheap rate electric, done last week's ironing and helped her mother have a bath, it was almost ten o'clock and the first chance she'd had all day to relax. Cassie made a large mug of coffee and settled on the sofa with Tony's book. Her plan to read and not think of Sam lasted all of two minutes. Whenever her mind was idle it worried about her son.

His latest girlfriend Lindy was big trouble. Sixteen going on twenty-five, her long, straight blonde hair and big blue eyes gave her an impression of innocence, but Cassie was convinced it was all a front. In fact Cassie was convinced the girl was messing with

Sam and enjoying a touch of 'bad boy' before she reverted to type. In ten years she'd be married to a doctor or lawyer and live in a large country home with her indulgent husband and two children. Occasionally she might remember the black-eyed boy she'd had a fling with before getting in her Mercedes SUV and driving to pick up her children from their private school.

Sam would be the one to get hurt but he wouldn't listen to Cassie's advice.

She sighed and opened the book, trailing her fingers over a beautiful photograph of a ring of standing stones. The words slowly drew her in until she jerked awake with a painful crick in her neck as the front door slammed.

Cassie sat up and tried to make out the time on her watch.

'Sam?'

He sloped in and stood, heavy-eyed with sadness, at the other end of the sofa.

Tentatively she held out her hand. 'Come and sit down.'

'I don't need another lecture,' he retorted.

Was that all she did? When had she last praised him for anything? But when had he done anything worth praising?

'No lecture. Just sit with me a while.'

Sam's thin body folded in as tightly as he could, as far away from her as possible.

'I was down the Green Dragon with Lindy.' His bottom lip stuck out, defensive and daring.

'Did you have a nice evening?'

He stared, puzzled. 'Nice? Aren't you going to give me the 'you're too young to drink' and 'Lindy's no good' speech?'

'What would be the point? I've told you so many times I'm worn out and it hasn't made any difference. You know the truth deep in here, Sam.' Her hand stretched across and rested against his thin cotton t-shirt, right on top of his thudding heart. For a fleeting moment, before he jumped back up to standing, his dark eyes glassed over with tears, oddly giving her hope, the first she'd felt in a long while.

'Sam. You can tell me anything, ask me anything, anytime.'

For a second he stopped, his shoulders falling in unspoken misery, but then his face closed down again and Sam walked away and headed upstairs. He'd always been a child to do things in his own time but Cassie wasn't sure she had the patience to keep on waiting.

\* \* \*

In her cold bedroom Cassie stripped and pulled on one of the old t-shirts she slept in, a worn pale blue with tiny holes under the arms, mended too many times. Jumping into bed she pulled the covers up in a desperate effort to warm up and indulged in a wide-awake daydream.

Cassie dropped her silk robe on the back of the elaborate white and gilt chair and stepped into the large marble bathtub. She lowered herself into the warm rose-scented water and lay back, resting her neck on a soft, pink velvet pillow. Rows of glowing candles illuminated the room and, within reach of her hand, a bottle of champagne sat on ice ready for her indulgence.

'Is there room for one more?'

Jay's soft, Irish lilt teased her senses as he stepped into the bathroom. He added his thick, white toweling robe to hers and turned, fixing her with his devilish silver blue eyes. Cassie's gaze roamed over his strong, muscular body and she gave a sly smile as his body reacted to her appraisal in an instant.

'I do believe there might be.'

She shifted forward in the huge tub, giving him room to get in behind her. He gently slid into the water and wrapped his long legs around her, rubbing against her until she gasped with a desperate need for more.

'Jay . . . Touch me . . . ' She looked over her shoulder and met his wicked grin as he slipped one hand around her hip and between her thighs and expertly teased her.

'Come for me, Cassie.'

His honeyed voice slid over her and she . . .

Cassie jerked upright in bed, suddenly cold again, but at least it stopped the exciting tremors running through her body.

She had to think about something other than Jay Burton. What to have for dinner tomorrow . . . the ironing . . . her unruly hair . . . boring things to send her to sleep.

It didn't work for long.

★ ★ ★

'There you go, Mr Burton, sir. All clean and ready to go. Nice day for a drive. Are you going far?' Brian Wood asked, holding out the car keys to Jay.

'Cornwall.'

Brian's heavy gray eyebrows shot towards the heavens and Jay suppressed a grin. He wasn't off to Outer Mongolia but the other man was a Londoner through to his bones so anywhere outside the M25 was 'the country' and not to be trusted.

'I'm visiting an old friend.'

Brian frowned. 'Well, you be careful, sir. I understand their roads aren't what we're used to.'

Jay didn't bother to say there were still white lines and traffic lights even when you got beyond Watford. 'I will and I promise to bring this baby back safely on Monday.'

Since the day he'd brought the car in to be entrusted to Brian Wood's tender care it had become a standing joke as to who was her owner. The man's job covered parking the cars and bringing them out again when residents requested, only cleaning vehicles if the resident paid extra, but Jay noticed his car's immaculate condition every time he drove it. The black metallic paint gleamed and the inside was always spotless and he guessed that the older man gave it a going over every day — and Jay was always interrogated, very politely, about where he was taking it and when it might be returned.

Driving alone was one of the joys of being single. Women, pets and children needed to be fed, watered and have frequent toilet breaks, and after a few miles women usually complained until he put the top up on the car so their hair didn't get messed.

Jay made Cornwall by noon, happier than he'd been in ages, and easily found the small shop tucked away behind the cathedral. He couldn't imagine how his friend made any money here, he thought as he flung open the door and walked in, immediately spotting Tony behind the counter.

'Got as far away from civilization as possible, have you?'

Tony beamed. 'You devil. I didn't expect you here yet. Suppose you burnt up the motorway with your petrol guzzling show-off of a car, did you?'

'You know me well. Come see her. She's a beauty.'

'Later, some of us have work to do.

You can drive us home tonight. It'll make a change from my trusty bicycle. My old car's been parked up so long it's probably seized up.'

'How about me treating you to lunch, then? I'm starved.'

'I bet you drove straight through, you idiot.'

Jay shrugged and flashed a quick smile.

'If a mug of tea or coffee will hold you for an hour or so then we'll eat at the Miner's Arms down the road. PG Tips or instant coffee — take your pick.'

'Tea, strong with a dash of milk and plenty sugar.'

Tony chuckled. 'So they haven't completely beaten the Irish out of you yet?'

Jay turned on his thickest accent, the one he wouldn't dare use around his fellow bankers at Solomon and Gates. 'Faith and begorrah, you're a useless eejit, so ye are.'

Tony rested a hand on Jay's arm, his

face suddenly serious. 'Glad you haven't changed too much.'

Jay couldn't speak. His friend was so wrong.

Tony called out towards the back of the shop. 'Hey, Cass, love, put the kettle on and come meet my weekend guest.'

Putting down the book he'd been idly looking at Jay turned around — and his heart thumped a missed beat in his chest.

'Cass, this is Jay Burton. He's the wild Irish boy I roomed with when I first went up to the wicked city to make my fortune. As you can see I ended up back here whereas he found the streets were paved with gold,' Tony said with good humor.

Jay's expectations for the weekend suddenly soared way up but the dark blue eyes he'd fantasised about hardened and glared as they looked at him as if he was a poisonous snake. Obviously she didn't share the same good memories of their day — and night — together.

Maybe all she needed was a touch of his special charm. 'Cassandra. It's so great to see you again. Have you worked with this rogue long?'

She remained mute and the uncomfortable silence made Tony stare from one to the other.

'You two know each other?'

Cassie's glare told Jay he'd better be very careful how he answered. 'We met briefly at Lake Garda last year. I'd taken my parents over for their Golden Wedding Anniversary.'

'I see.' Tony obviously didn't want it spelled out any further. He hadn't forgotten Jay's reputation with women.

'I've been here about a month,' Cassie grudgingly answered. 'I'll just go and make the tea.'

'Riled her up did you?' Tony asked when she left the room. 'She doesn't seem thrilled to see you again. That must be a first, Mr Casanova.'

'Oh, you know women. It was a holiday thing. I thought she'd understood that.' Jay tried to give the impression of complete disinterest.

Cassie returned and placed two mugs on the counter.

'I'll take my lunch break now if that's OK, Tony. I'll be back by one.' When Tony nodded she almost ran from the room.

Jay unconsciously followed her form, his eyes lingering on her neat curves and pert backside.

'Hey, I haven't seen that look before,' Tony observed. 'Got to you, did she? Or is it just that she's a challenge because she's not interested?'

Jay wasn't about to answer, so quickly changed the subject. 'Why don't you tell me what you've been up to? Last I heard you were trekking with a load of goat herders in Tibet.'

They easily slipped back into their old way of conversation, but Jay was weighed down with a sadness he couldn't explain as memories flooded back . . .

Two young men with their wild plans and schemes. Jay had planned to make big money in a few years, help his family, and quit. He'd lead an expedition to Everest and do philanthropic work in poor communities in that part of the world. Tony would be the next Laurence Olivier, winning multiple Oscars for his creative roles, feted by the Hollywood elite, and always appearing with a different A-list actress on his arm.

Judging by the cramped shop and Tony's simple lifestyle things hadn't worked out quite like that for him either.

Tony's sharp, green eyes pinned Jay's thoughts to the floor. 'I couldn't be happier. There's nothing else I need. Well, I wouldn't turn down the right woman but apart from that . . . '

'What about your acting?'

'That was boyish nonsense. Travel and immersing myself in other cultures gave me clarity. There's very little a person needs to be truly content. If I can be happy with less someone else can have a better life and I'm good with that. I act in local amateur productions to satisfy my craving for the spotlight.'

Jay couldn't reconcile this serious, thoughtful, mature man with the flamboyant, handsome young man ready to set the world on fire. Thinking too introspectively wasn't something Jay cared to indulge in.

'Hey, Cassie's back,' Tony said, although Jay already knew because her light, floral fragrance filled the room. 'Let's go eat. You can catch me up on all your news.'

Jay forced a smile as she met his gaze full on and stared right into him, dissected what she saw and then coolly turned away from him as if she found him wanting.

Who did she think she was? Damned woman.

# 3

Cassie only had to get through the afternoon and they'd be closed for the rest of the Easter weekend. But the Irish devil watched her continually. A carefree smile touching his generous mouth and his mesmerising eyes swallowed her whole.

If he thought she was gullible enough to fall for his charm again he was wrong.

'Why don't you join Jay and me for dinner tonight?' Tony asked innocently. 'I thought we might eat at the Hunter's Arms. You said the other day you wanted to go there and it's close to home for you.'

She hesitated, hating to refuse Tony. He was kind and one of her few friends.

'Please. I need rescuing from this hard-drinking wretch.'

Cassie dared a quick glance at Jay

but all he did was raise one eyebrow and twist his smile a shade more temptingly.

'I really can't. I have to cook dinner for my parents and they've been on their own all day.' As if they wanted any conversation with her. The three of them would sit and watch TV while her mother criticised everything and everybody.

Tony dropped down on one knee, snatched her hands in his, and threw his head back dramatically. 'Oh lovely lady, take pity on us poor men. Don't leave us in despairing loneliness.'

Against her will Cassie burst out laughing.

'I'm glad to see your acting talents are still alive and well, old friend.' Jay's wry words were full of good humor.

'Acting. You mean all that was fake?' Cassie couldn't resist joining in the friendly banter.

'Didn't you know your illustrious boss once trod the boards of the best London theatres? When he wasn't sweeping them that is,' Jay said lightheartedly.

'Is that so?' She wasn't sure how much Jay was making up.

Tony threw them both a haughty, disdainful look. 'Heathens. You don't appreciate genius. Yes, Cassie love, I once aspired to follow in the footsteps of Olivier, but fate conspired otherwise.'

Jay's rich, deep laugh resonated in the small space. 'Ask him about his experience in a Greek costume. Attracted the girls and got us free gyros for a week, a big bonus to a couple of penniless, starving, young men.'

'That's enough. I retract the invitation, Cassie,' Tony declared. 'Stay home and eat beans on toast with your parents and watch the Eurovision song contest for all I care. It'll be suitable torture for an unappreciative young woman.'

Cassie gave up and smiled broadly straight at Jay, wishing the brilliant smile she received in return didn't make her heart flip. 'Oh, alright. I'll break my parents' hearts and join you.'

Tony dropped a friendly kiss on her cheek but Jay only stood back and watched, his eyes gleaming with interest, his mouth a firm unreadable line.

Wrong decision, Cassie thought — again.

★ ★ ★

Both men stood to greet her and two sets of admiring eyes told her the red blouse was the wrong choice, although it had seemed innocuous enough in her bedroom. A softly draping shirt, with a ruffle falling around a modest v-neck, paired with black linen trousers — nothing out of the ordinary.

Cassie leant in towards Tony, allowing his lips to brush her cheek. His long glossy blonde hair was loose tonight and he'd abandoned his usual scruffy jeans and t-shirt for tight black leather trousers, a black cotton shirt and a wide black belt with an ornate silver buckle.

Unsettled, she turned to greet Jay.

41

Another woman might be fooled by his bland expression but the unique liquid silver blue shading in his eyes, emphasised by lethally long dark lashes, was anything but bland. He stepped closer and rested his lips briefly on the skin of her temple. The searing mark he left behind would no doubt burn the rest of the night. A dark, musky scent clung to his skin making her yearn to step in even closer.

Cassie almost stumbled as Jay pulled out a chair for her, flinching from the touch of his hand as he steadied her.

'I'll get us some menus. What'll you have to drink, Cassie?' Tony asked and her breathing slowly steadied.

'Chardonnay, please.'

Jay angled his chair and extended his long legs into her space. Cassie wished he wasn't as handsome in real life as he always appeared in her dreams. His immaculately cut smooth, dark hair contrasted perfectly with his lightly tanned skin. No man around here could pair worn jeans, a pale pink shirt and black leather ankle boots, but on him it worked. He might be a banker but he was no lightweight apology for a man. The way his jeans pulled over his well-muscled thighs and the breadth of his shoulders indicated someone with a healthy respect for his own body. Cassie desperately strived not to recall what an amazing body it was.

Tony held out a glass of wine inches from her face and she blushed, wondering how long he'd stood there.

'Our food will be here soon. Cheers.'

They all raised their glasses in a toast but Cassie was sure she was the only one wishing the evening would be over soon.

A little later, Cassie sat back, full of the most delicious spaghetti carbonara and relished the novelty of not having to hurry up and wash the dishes. She listened quietly as the men rehashed their shared past. Tony's stories revealed a softer Jay, close to his large Irish family and full of fun. Jay said little, not contradicting but almost as though he couldn't stand to be reminded of his younger self.

'You grew up here didn't you, Cassie?' Tony asked and she fiddled with her glass, unsure how to reply. Sam and her past weren't up for discussion.

'What's the cottage you've renovated like?' Jay asked Tony, smoothly changing the subject. She was grateful but hated to think he'd guessed at her reluctance.

'Dessert, coffee, brandy? What do you fancy, Cassie?'

She determined to give Tony a simple reply to what was surely an innocent question. 'Black coffee would be great.'

Jay nodded. 'Same for me.'

When Tony headed to the bar Jay slid into the chair next to Cassie and his hand lifted to her hair where one finger strayed to pick up a curl, gently pulling it straight before letting go.

'Don't think you've got away,' he said. 'I don't give up.'

'You did last year. You only get one chance.'

To her surprise he grinned and moved back to his own seat as Tony returned to join them. They drank their coffee and Cassie plotted her escape.

'I need to go. Thanks very much for a lovely evening.'

Tony jumped to his feet. 'We'll give you a lift. You're not walking home at this late hour.'

'I'll be fine. You two stay and talk some more, I'm sure you've a lot to catch up on. I'll see you on Tuesday after the holiday, Tony. And Jay . . . ' His attention focused on her and her lips tangled around the words she wanted to say.

A sudden comotion diverted her attention.

'I've told you lot before. I don't care if other places serve you, you're underage and I'm not risking my license.' The landlord was trying to get rid of a loud bunch of teenagers who'd just piled into the pub.

'Sam?' Cassie's heart sunk.

'Mum?

A frisson of shock settled on Jay's face as he looked at the heavily pierced, shaven-headed boy who was wavering on his feet in front of them, and connected him with Cassie.

'That boy is yours?'

Cassie was certain she heard contempt in his voice. The teenagers shouted and swore as they swaggered out of the door and Tony gently pulled at Cassie's arm to sit her back down.

'Let him go. I'll take you home when you're a bit steadier,' Tony said then turned to Jay and added, 'Go get Cassie a brandy, would you?'

When Jay returned, Tony took the glass from Jay and held it to her lips. After a few small sips the dreadful tightness inside her eased. Jay still didn't speak.

'Bring the car over to the door and I'll walk out with Cassie.' Tony wouldn't listen to her attempt at a protest.

Settling her in the front, Tony clambered into the cramped back seat

46

while Cassie pulled herself together enough to give Jay directions, but that was the sum total of their conversation.

Outside her house she noticed Jay's large hands as they gripped the steering wheel, the tight line of his jaw. She couldn't blame him.

★  ★  ★

Jay watched the sunrise from the kitchen window while his coffee grew cold. He didn't immediately turn to face his friend when he walked into the room.

'Did you know?' he asked.

'Know what? That Cassie had a son and what her son was like?' Tony asked.

Jay shrugged.

'It's not your business any more than it's mine but no, I didn't. She's a very private person and doesn't talk much about her family. I know she lives with her parents but they don't get on too well. I assume she didn't tell you about the boy when you . . . when

47

you met before?'

A rush of heat flooded Jay's neck. 'We didn't spend much time talking.'

'I'd never have guessed.'

'I'm sorry Tony, I . . . '

'It's not me you need to apologise to.'

Jay shook his head. 'Yeah, like I don't know that but it's pretty obvious how she'll react if I call.'

'It's your own fault. I suggest you leave it for now. Anything in particular you want to do today?'

Jay couldn't think straight. He kept seeing Cassie's sad, tired eyes as they registered her son's behavior; resignation, not shock, as if she'd seen it too many times.

It wasn't like Jay could be any real help; he'd be gone on Monday so logically it'd be best to leave her alone.

'Haven't got a clue. You're the local. Take me somewhere interesting.' Jay flexed his arms and stretched. 'Maybe a walk on your famous cliffs, anything to work off some energy.'

Tony nodded. They'd always been

well clued in to each other's moods and he'd missed that without even realising it.

'I don't suppose you have hiking boots with you? I mean ones that've actually been worn rather than bought for show.'

Jay punched Tony's arm. 'Yeah, I have actually — and since when have you turned into a hardcore outdoor fiend? Walking to the pub used to be the extent of your exercise.'

'People change, Jay. Even you.'

A heavy, knowing silence filled the room.

'I'll cook us breakfast then we'll take your fancy car to Camelford on Bodmin Moor. A strenuous hike up to the top of Rough Tor and back should do the trick for your restless spirit.'

Jay kept his mouth shut at Tony's accurate summing up.

\* \* \*

Jay scrambled up the last granite slab to reach the top, turned and gave Tony a satisfied smile. Proving he didn't merely lead a soft London life felt good. Work colleagues and girlfriends were used to him disappearing off for occasional weekends. They'd be surprised to find out he went climbing in the Lake District. Although never quite acknowledging it substituted for Ireland in his head, it kept him this side of sane.

He sucked in a deep breath of clear air and dutifully looked at all the places Tony pointed out. Brown Willy, the highest point in Cornwall a few miles in one direction and the Bronze Age settlement they'd passed on the way up in the other — but his heart saw Cloghernagh from the top of Lugnaquillia last time he'd climbed it with Eamon.

'Ready to head back down?'

'Definitely,' Jay said. 'Don't know about you but I'm ready for a pint.' If it wasn't for the car Jay would've renewed his friendship with the whiskey bottle. They walked back in silence as they headed for the nearest pub.

'I didn't mean it the way it sounded.' Jay tried to explain once they'd got their drinks. 'About Cassie's son, I mean.'

'Maybe but you know as well as I do that you came across as a judgmental asshole.'

Jay couldn't argue against the accuracy of Tony's statement.

'I was horrified *for* Cassie, not at her. I couldn't believe that was her life, what she was dealing with every day.'

'I don't think she's going to believe you, mate.' Tony scoffed.

Jay swallowed the rest of his pint and slammed the glass down on the table. 'Why should I care if she does or not?'

His friend shot him a pitying look. 'Do you really want me to spell out the obvious?'

'You're crazy. I barely know the woman. And she's not my type anyway,' Jay insisted. He purposely chose what to say next, prefering to cement Tony's low view of him rather than have him think he cared. 'Hey, she was good in

51

bed, but I don't need a harassed single mother with a delinquent son to get laid.'

Tony didn't speak; the scorn in his eyes spoke for him. Jay should've been pleased but a sick emptiness settled in his gut.

'Let's go back to your place. I'll probably leave in the morning. I've got a client I should be doing some work for so I might take advantage of the time off to catch up.' Jay declared.

For a moment Tony hesitated with only a bare approximation of a smile. 'Whatever you want,' he said as he picked up his backpack and headed towards the door.

The next day Tony helped Jay load his car. 'Come back soon,' he said with the ghost of a smile.

Jay didn't think he should be forgiven so easily but Tony always had a higher opinion of him than he did of himself. 'Would you tell Cassie . . . ?'

'I'm not telling her anything. That's down to you. Write to her if you can't talk on the phone. You know that thing people used to do. Get some proper paper and write an apology, put a stamp on it and put it in a postbox. Hell, I bet that posh place you live in has a doorman who would post it for you.'

Jay flushed at Tony's sharp observations about his life. The sooner he put the craziness of this weekend behind him the better. As if he was going to scribble a groveling apology to a woman he'd never see again.

* * *

Cassie heard something fall through the letter box and wandered out to the door to pick up the newspaper. An envelope lay on the ugly brown carpet and she stared at the unfamiliar writing. No stamp, just her name scrawled in thick, black ink on cream colored, good quality paper. Her eyes leaped down to the signature. Jay Burton.

*I must apologise for my terrible manners last night. It was never my intention to offend you. I hope you'll believe me, although I don't expect your forgiveness.*

*I understand now we had different views on where our previous meeting might lead, but I hope you won't let that stand in the way if I can ever do anything to help you. I'm enclosing one of my business cards with a contact phone number, so please call if you need me.*

*If I'm ever in Cornwall again I hope we can meet as friends.*

*Sincerely*
*Jay Burton*


Arrogant jerk! How much more condescending could the man be? Cassie's shaking fingers crumpled up the paper and card and tossed them in the direction of the rubbish bin.

How could she face going to work on Tuesday? She wasn't sure which had been worse — the revulsion in Jay's eyes or the pity in Tony's.

The phone started to ring and stopped her musing. Please don't let it be another problem, she thought as she picked it up.

'Peter Retallick here, Lindy's father. Where the devil's your son taken my girl off to?' His anger pulsed down the line.

'What are you talking about?' Cassie asked, confused.

'For goodness sake, woman, it's a simple question! My daughter is missing and she left a note saying she and Sam had gone off together. Apparently we weren't appreciative enough when she took up with your lay-about, drugged up son. According to her he's the perfect boyfriend for a beautiful, well-educated doctor's daughter set to go to Oxford.' His sarcasm poured down the line straight into Cassie's heart.

'I assumed he was at your house with Lindy,' she ventured.

'You don't seriously believe we'd

allow him to stay here overnight, do you?'

Cassie stiffened. 'He's returned several mornings and claimed that's where he'd been. I assumed you preferred them to be together under your roof rather than elsewhere. I'm afraid Sam stopped listening to me a long time ago . . . I — '

'I've no interest in your lack of parenting skills. All I care about is my daughter. I'm calling the police, so you should expect a visit from them very soon.'

Cassie struggled to stay calm. 'I understand your worry but the police won't show a lot of interest in two sixteen-year-olds who've run away from — '

'That might be true in your son's case but it's not so with Lindy. Her godfather is the Chief Constable for Devon and Cornwall, her grandfather is a retired judge and two of her uncles are barristers. She will be found.'

'I'm just as worried about my son as

you are about Lindy. I'll call around his friends, see if anyone knows anything. I'll call you back if I — '

'Fine. But expect the police to turn up on your doorstep.'

'Just for a change.' Cassie spoke the words into an empty phone. She could call Jay and ask for his help, she thought bitterly. What a joke that would be, though it'd be interesting to hear his reaction after his pathetic, so called apology.

Perversely it was a beautiful day with a soft breeze blowing and sunshine lighting up the daffodils swaying outside the window. Cassie forced herself to keep busy and put the beef in the oven for lunch, and while it was cooking she worked through the ironing pile. This afternoon she'd clean the house to keep from thinking.

She picked up the crumpled remains of Jay's letter, all set to make sure it went in the bin this time, but at the last second she did an odd, unexplainable thing. Cassie straightened out the small

card and slipped it into her jeans
pocket.

* * *

'Who's that?' Cassie's mother snapped
at the sound of the front doorbell.

She smoothed down her hair and
tried to smile. 'I don't know. I could
answer the door and find out, if you
like.'

'That's enough of your smart tongue,
young lady,' her mother snapped back.
'I don't like having my Sunday
disturbed.'

Cassie ignored her and walked out
into the hall, just able to make out two
large shapes through the frosted glass.
They hadn't taken long.

'Ms Moore? We'd like to speak to
your son.' The young policeman made
no effort to be pleasant.

Her fury, at a slow simmer over the
last couple of days, finally erupted.
Cassie was tired of being treated like a
second-class citizen. 'He's not here,

which I'm sure Doctor Retallick informed you before you came.'

The older man, gray and rumpled, spoke softly. 'I'm Detective Inspector Paul Harris. Could we come in? We're only interested in the welfare of these two young people.'

Cassie shrugged and stood back to let them pass.

'Police?' Cassie's mother said as soon as the two men appeared. 'What's that no-good boy done now? He's a disgrace to this family.'

'Mother, please be quiet. Sam's gone off with Lindy.'

'He's probably got her in the club — runs in the family,' she said with a sneer.

Paul Harris touched Cassie's arm. 'Is there somewhere we can talk in private?'

'Follow me.' She led the way into the kitchen and closed the door behind them. Cassie stood and folded her arms. 'I want to help but I honestly don't know where they are. At least

Lindy's parents got a note.'

'I know they're over sixteen but there are claims Sam might've coerced Lindy. There's talk of drugs being involved.'

Cassie straightened up and met his questioning eyes head on. 'Sam's no angel, I'm the first to admit that. He drinks, he smokes and he's probably dabbled in pot, but I'd swear he doesn't do anything worse. Don't let them tell you Lindy's Little Miss Perfect. She pursued Sam in the first place and was already on the pill when he started going with her. Sam told me when I asked if he was being careful.'

The younger policeman's harsh green eyes pinned her down. 'That's not the story her family told us.'

'None of us want to think our kids aren't perfect, do we?' Cassie returned. 'The difference is I had to admit it years ago.'

'Can we look in Sam's room?' The detective asked. 'We can get a warrant, but it's easier this way.'

'Who for?' Cassie snipped back. 'Oh,

what's the point. Go ahead. Top of the stairs on your right.'

They found nothing and after they'd gone Cassie sat alone. She flipped Jay's card over and over before she shoved it back in her pocket. She'd manage without anyone — same as usual.

★　★　★

*Another one bites the dust*, Jay thought philosophically.

Annabelle caught him in bed with Naomi and dumped him. Naomi had fluttered her fake eyelashes at him for ages at work and last night he'd stupidly succumbed, although goodness knows why. For a supposedly intelligent woman she had the conversational style of a trained monkey. He hated it when women gazed adoringly and agreed with everything he said.

His brother, Eamon, had predicted one night that Jay would only settle down when he found the one woman who didn't bore him. He'd replied arrogantly, 'They all do.'

But it was a lie . . .

Dark blue eyes fiery with disdain . . . uncontrolled blonde curls itching to be stroked and tamed . . . a subtly luscious body, responsive as hell . . . bright, funny, sexy.

Cassie didn't bore him.

Nothing had gone right since his weekend in Cornwall.

He'd lost an important client at work because he hadn't paid close enough attention to the market, then some moron had backed into his car at the opera last week.

The tears in Brian's eyes when he saw it shut Jay's mouth on what he'd been going to say — that it didn't really matter, it was only a car. A car worth over a hundred thousand pounds, but only a car when all was said and done.

Jay poured an inch of neat whiskey into his glass and knocked it back in one swallow. The instant shot of warmth hit his empty stomach with a welcome punch. He tried to remember if he'd eaten today but gave up bothering.

Another drink followed that one, and then another.

* * *

Ferocious sunlight pounded Jay's eyes until he managed to drag them half open and struggled to focus on his watch. Nine o'clock. Great. Late for work on top of everything else.

Showered and dressed, Jay checked his phone while he poured a second cup of pitch black tea.

Six messages. Iona's first, then his other siblings and finally his father. The acid rolling around Jay's stomach twisted it into painful coils. He sucked in a deep breath before listening to the first and without stopping heard each in turn. Only when he got to his father's broken voice did his tears fall.

While he'd been passed out drunk, his mother had died.

The fact he couldn't have got there in

time didn't matter somehow. Why had no-one even told him she was ill?

He dialed Eamon's number.

'She went quiet, Pat. Da's grieving somethin' awful. You'll come right away.'

There was no question and Jay was grateful someone trusted that he could be relied on.

# 4

Two hours later Jay was at Heathrow. He'd probably screwed his career by telling John Gates, his Eton-educated boss, to go to hell. The moron had told Jay he should put his clients first and there was an important meeting he apparently dared not miss. Jay lost it when Gates generously told him to take a couple of days off, even though the funeral was not until next week. Jay's reply got him a lecture and a stern warning.

He didn't speak to the elderly woman next to him on the plane because she resembled his mother too much, with her tight gray perm, tweed skirt, matching wool sweater and sensible brown leather shoes. She clutched nervously at her overstuffed handbag but he couldn't reassure her. Not today.

When he finally arrived in Ireland,

Jay spotted his brother in the small crowd gathered around new arrivals.

'Over here, Pat lad,' Eamon called out and stepped close to pull Jay into his embrace, the lingering scent of stale smoke and mothballs rose from the black coat he wore when anyone died.

A layer peeled from Jay's façade.

When they got back to the house, Deirdre, Iona, Siobhan and Colum surrounded him and each took their turns, peeling away more layers of emotion. By the time he walked into the kitchen and faced his father, Jay was stripped raw.

'I'm here. Da.'

'Aye, I knew you'd come. I wanted to tell you she weren't well but she wouldn't have it. Said you were too busy. Said she'd be alright, she did.'

Jay could hardly bear to meet his father's brimming eyes, full of love, no condemnation. Overnight Connor Burton, at nearly eighty, had become an old man. For fifty-five years he'd worshipped his precious Ailene. There'd never been a cross word heard by their children. Sure, they'd disagreed but they always ended up smiling and kissing each other to make up.

'Your Aunt Mary's with your mother. In the best room. I . . . '

'I'll go in with him, Da.' Eamon rested a hand on his father's trembling shoulders and led Jay away.

\* \* \*

It was damn near impossible to get away from them all. They'd done their usual smothering act, taking care of their baby brother, until finally, by three in the morning, they'd all drifted away to their homes or fallen asleep in the old house.

It was too dark to walk far but the moon cast a faint glow and the stars filled the sky, unblemished by city lights. Jay walked briskly to the end of their land, resting on a stone wall he'd helped his father repair years ago. Through his pocket his fingers traced

67

over the shape of the flask Eamon had slipped in there but it didn't tempt him.

Father O'Connell had the funeral arranged for Monday. Five long days to get through. Jay guessed it would be out of line to suggest a climb to Eamon, but he craved the physical exertion. He had the notion it'd be a more real honoring of their mother than any church service. She'd always loved the fact her boys enjoyed nothing better than pitting themselves against the Irish hills. He couldn't imagine getting on the plane Tuesday morning and going back to London. Back to his old life.

What would happen if he didn't? He certainly wouldn't starve any time soon but he couldn't stay here.

An idea sneaked in. Tony mentioned never having any time off since he opened the shop and Jay had a ton of holidays built up that he hadn't used — so why not take some? He'd offer to help run the book shop for a few weeks to give him some thinking time and help his friend.

Cassie might not care for the idea but maybe she'd come to see a better side of him. She couldn't see much worse, that was for sure.

Jay stared out into the night and shivered. He'd never been one for the whole Irish second sight thing, only believing what he saw with his eyes, but his mother was with him now as surely as she ever had been.

'Did you know I needed to be home? I'm lost, Ma. Help me.'

Jay's words shivered in the breeze. Talking to her was as natural as it ever had been. A smooth hand seemed to brush away his tears and a sense of peace swept over him.

\* \* \*

Cassie shivered in the cool early April sun. She'd brought a sandwich and her heartache to the small park by the cathedral. Something about being in the shadow of the imposing granite building always seemed to reassure her and today she could do with some comfort.

Her worries piled up like a badly balanced stack of books. There were no leads on Sam and Lindy. Her mother's arthritis was worse and hospital appointments meant days missed at work, something they couldn't afford. The edges of her life were held together by the merest sliver of control.

On the grass a small boy played with a ball, his blonde hair shining in the thin sun. He dropped the ball and ran over to his mother, flinging his chubby, toddler arms around the lucky woman. She wouldn't realise how lucky she was because it was one of those taken-for-granted moments.

Sam had been an innocent little boy once, too.

Cassie wanted to scream at people who stared at Sam, making rude comments about his appearance and behavior. She ached to tell them what a loving child he'd been — and still was underneath. In her heart Cassie knew the piercings, tattoos, and shaved head were nothing more than a cry for help.

'Cassie, love. Are you alright?' She raised her face to Tony, startled by his anxiety. 'It was getting late. I was concerned about you. It's two o'clock, Cassie.'

Cassie slapped her hand to her mouth in horror. Now she'd lose her job on top of everything else! 'Oh! I'm so sorry. I don't know what . . . I wasn't . . . '

Tony's warm hands enveloped hers as he said, 'I'm not mad. I was worried. You're always so prompt, that's all. Come on let's walk back together.'

She didn't mind when he slipped his arm through hers.

Opening the shop door he stared at her and Cassie couldn't decipher the meaning behind his clear green eyes. He leaned in closer and she caught her breath, certain he was going to kiss her and wondered how to react. Cassie smelt his familiar lime soap and her hand strayed upwards to stroke his jaw.

71

His lips brushed her cheek before he stepped back and she couldn't decide whether to be disappointed or not.

'Cassie. I've put off telling you this because you won't like it, but it'll only be for a couple of weeks and . . . oh hell, I'm getting ahead of myself, but well, you see, I haven't had a holiday since I bought the shop four years ago.'

'You want to close for a week or two? That's OK.' It wasn't really because she couldn't expect him to pay her but Cassie put on an accommodating smile.

'No, I'm not going to close, but would you be able to do a few more hours? Someone's coming to help you run the place while I'm away . . . Jay Burton, actually . . . '

Surprising both Tony and herself, Cassie burst out laughing.

'Why on earth would your hotshot banker friend want to be stuck here?'

'He offered. He wants a break from London but he said he won't come if you object.'

There had to be more behind Jay's

offer than kindness, but she couldn't voice her concern. He'd known she couldn't object when Tony was so kind to her.

'It's fine with me. Where are you planning on going?' She doubted she'd fooled Tony with her studied casualness.

'I'm not sure yet. Some friends are off to Australia and they've asked me to go along. Of course if I do it might be more than two weeks. Jay said to take as long as I wanted but . . . '

'Go, it's fine. Have a good time.' Cassie took a deep breath and dragged up a bright smile. 'When's Jay arriving?'

'He'll drive down on Sunday and stay at my place. I'll take a day or two to show him the ropes and I'd like to be off no later than Wednesday.'

They were both adults. This wouldn't be a problem. They'd work together for a couple of weeks and then go their separate ways again. Simple.

\* \* \*

This was stupid. Why was it taking so long to make up her mind what to wear on an ordinary Monday morning? She didn't have many clothes to choose from and certainly didn't want Jay Burton thinking she'd made any kind of special effort.

Cassie had wasted most of yesterday with fruitless phone calls to Sam's so-called friends. They all claimed not to have heard from him but were about as trustworthy as he was.

'Cassandra. The bus won't wait for you,' her mother carped.

She quickly pulled a yellow, flowery t-shirt on with her usual jeans. There was no time for make-up now anyway so the decision was made for her. Why were buses never late when you wanted them to be?

When she got there Jay's low, lilting voice drifted through the shop and Cassie's chest tightened. The first day by the hotel pool she'd known she could listen to him forever. He could recite a grocery list in his soft, Irish accent and she'd melt — but she was determined that no way would he guess by her reactions.

'Good morning. Good weekend, Tony? Hello Jay, I bet you didn't expect to be back here so soon?'

Cassie forced the blush back down her neck as both men's eyes turned on her. 'I'll go to the back and sort the new books.'

Theory was one thing, practice another. Cassie sighed. It was going to be a long morning.

* * *

'Why don't you and Jay go to lunch while I finish the accounts? I must get them straight before I leave.'

The challenge in Tony's quirky smile stopped her protest; he wanted to make sure she could handle this.

Cassie led the way to the pub, purposely staying far enough ahead that they couldn't speak.

While Jay went to the bar to fetch

their drinks she studied him. Earlier she couldn't put her finger on what was different but now it came to her. There was no humor dancing on his lips, no sparkle in his eyes and none of the usual energy bursting from him. Even the dark trousers and burgundy shirt he wore today were subdued.

She glanced around and noted she wasn't the only woman watching him, but he was oblivious.

Halfway through her scampi and chips she noticed him staring at his untouched plate.

'It's not that bad. I know it's not gourmet city cuisine but it'll keep you going for a heavy afternoon of book selling.'

A slight smile creased his face before immmediately fading away. 'I'm not hungry.'

Cassie barely caught his whispered words but they made her look closer. Usually lean and muscular, today he verged on thin. His blue in his eyes had faded, leaving behind a solemn silvery gray. Reaching across the table she impulsively rested her hand on top of his.

'What's wrong, Jay? You don't look well.'

He dropped his gaze to the plate but not before she saw a film of tears pressing at his eyes. 'Nothing. I'm fine.'

Yeah, right and I'm the Queen of Sheba, but for now she'd let Jay get away with the lie.

'This'll make you laugh.' Jay's bright grin was forced. 'A young policeman stopped me for speeding on the motorway yesterday but one look at the BMW's engine and he was lost. It was all he could do not to drool. Let me off with a warning.' He chuckled and finished off his drink in one swallow.

Cassie dutifully joined in but knew it didn't reach her eyes.

'We'd better get back and rescue Tony. Math was never his strong point. I'll give him a hand with sorting it out.'

'Good idea.'

He let her get up first, and Cassie

was pretty sure his eyes were on her all the way back — he might be sad about something but he wasn't dead yet.

* * *

Jay stretched out his long legs, grateful his tall friend had indulged in a king-size bed. He glanced around the very spare, clean room with its stark, white painted walls. Years ago Tony's bedroom was a notorious den of iniquity draped with dramatic, Indian fabrics and redolent with burning incense, all the better for seduction. Today's bed was covered in a plain blue quilt and the only other furniture was a simple dresser, chair and wardrobe, picked up at second-hand sales judging by the worn, scratched wood.

Jay pulled up the white, wide-slatted, blinds and opened the window, pleasantly startled as cool air hit his bare skin.

Why hadn't he told Tony about his mother? Did the act of speaking it out loud make it too real? He'd left Dublin as soon as he could, promised to return soon and seen the disappointment in his family's eyes.

They'd heard it all before.

Eamon was the only one with the courage to say what he needed to hear. 'You can only go on running so long, Pat. She knew it. We know it. You'll get it sometime, boy.'

Cassie knows it too. She knows I'm running. He couldn't decide how the knowledge of her understanding made him feel. If he could sleep and forget it all for even one night it would help but his body jangled with stress and un-spent energy. In London he'd go to a nightclub, pick up an anonymous girl, but there was nowhere to do that here.

A clear memory of Cassie appeared in the fading moonlight, her blonde curls spread over the pillow, sapphire eyes glittering with pleasure and her lush, pink lips smiling teasingly at him . . .

'You going to give me your phone

number, darlin' girl?'

'I might consider it if you're very good,' she'd said.

'You mean I haven't been good enough already?'

His teasing words made her visibly shiver, and as he had dragged his gaze down over her an excited flush made her skin glow enticingly.

'Would you like me to be really good again?' he'd drawled, teasing his fingers down to her breast before following it with his mouth. Jay drew circles with his tongue and nipped and sucked at the tender skin.

'If you must.' She'd tried to sound as if she was doing him a favor and gave a smug smile as he obeyed, losing them both for a while longer.

He had lain sprawled over the bed, completely spent from their loving and watched her dress.

Cassie had retrieved a piece of paper from her bag and scribbled down her name and number. He took it with a smile and tossed it on the bedside table before kissing her goodbye.

In her expressive eyes he'd seen her recognise something in him that he preferred to hide. In reaction to that look he had screwed up the piece of paper and thrown it in the bin before starting to pack.

Now he'd deliberately put himself back in her orbit and a sliver of apprehension snaked through him, mixed with a definite desire for another chance with Cassie.

Jay rolled out of bed and pulled on his discarded jeans. He strode into the living room and fired up his laptop. While it purred into action he poured himself a large glass of whiskey with a splash of water.

Work and whiskey. His never fail remedies for insomnia and disturbing women.

* * *

He was good at this. It didn't matter if it was a famous merchant bank in the centre of London or a small bookshop in a backstreet of a Cornish town, the principles were the same and he'd grasped them young. Give people what they want, money or books, and they'll come back for more.

Cassie half-heartedly protested a few of his suggestions but when he dragged out some of her own she lit up; clearly nobody had ever given her the kind of support he'd taken for granted from his family. Sixteen-year-old Jay had informed his father he'd be a millionaire by the time he was twenty-five and Connor Burton never even cracked a smile. He'd asked serious questions and done whatever he could to help it come true, even though Jay was certain it was a dream he never shared.

Cassie's first suggestion of a corner with comfy chairs where people could sit and read and have a free cup of coffee worked its magic within days. She rearranged the window displays to be more eye-catching, tempting in people who normally never stepped foot in a book shop.

Jay's biggest surprise was himself; he hadn't read anything but financial stuff for years but discovered he got a kick from opening a new delivery and coming across something that caught his imagination. Today's find was a slim volume on Celtic myths. Cassie grinned when she caught him lounging in one of the new chairs, engrossed in the legend of King Arthur.

'Cornwall getting its claws into you, is it? Don't you have enough of your own Irish legends?' she teased.

'I never paid much attention to them. It all sounded like a bunch of fairy tales to me and I suppose this is the same.'

'You skeptic. Don't go telling the customers it's all made up. That's not good salesmanship.'

Her tantalising smile drifted from her eyes to her mouth and back again. He was sure she'd be horrified if he blurted out how badly he ached to kiss her. He'd blown his chance long ago and screwed up again over the whole incident with her son. Cassie wasn't a woman to easily change her mind — but Jay wasn't renowned to be stubborn without reason. One week of Tony's holiday was gone already and Jay guessed he had about two more to work his magic.

Time to make a move.

'You got any plans tonight, darlin',' Jay caught her blush as he slipped back into his natural way of speaking.

'Let me see. The house is a mess, I haven't had time to do the washing — oh, and we haven't had meals that aren't from a tin or the freezer all week. How will that do for a start?'

He stood and walked over to the counter, leaned on his elbows and stared blatantly at her.

'Keep me company for dinner tonight. It's no fun eatin' alone. You choose where and when.'

In the seconds before she answered Jay vividly recalled being fifteen and asking a girl out for the first time; the paralysing fear of being rejected mixed with the almost bigger fear of being accepted and wondering what the hell to do next.

Cassie frowned and Jay's heart sunk way down his legs, pooling by his feet until he was sure he wouldn't be able to walk.

'I'm not sure.'

She probably wanted him to assure her it was only as work colleagues, that he had no ulterior motives, but he wouldn't lie.

Jay straightened and stretched his arms out, resting one hand very deliberately on each of her shoulders. They trembled under his fingers — or was he the one shaking?

'Please.'

He'd never pleaded with any woman, never needed to.

The tip of her tongue slipped out to lick her lips. Were they dry with nerves, or was he projecting his own feelings onto her?

'I shouldn't but I suppose I can't risk

losing my job, so alright.' Her words were light and full of laughter and he grinned.

Closing time couldn't come soon enough. Jay crossed his fingers and hoped he wasn't the only one thinking that.

# 5

*This is a reward for your hard work this week. No, it isn't. It's because he wants you back in his bed. Don't be silly. It's no different than going out with Jay and Tony together. If you think that you're dafter than I gave you credit for.*

The annoying conversation in her head wouldn't stop and it'd been driving her crazy ever since she'd agreed to have dinner with Jay. The 'what to wear' discussion started next.

*Keep your jeans on and add a clean shirt. Slink into that cute, blue skirt you've never worn, show him you're no yokel. Go for an ordinary summer dress with a cardigan, a slight effort but not too sexy. For goodness sake act like a woman for once. You remember what that is, don't you?*

Cassie ripped off her work clothes and stood for ages under the hot shower. After drying off she rubbed in plenty of the indulgent magnolia scented lotion she'd bought herself for Christmas. The skirt, blue and flirty as a field of cornflowers, slipped on easily. It was far too short for a thirty-two-year old mother but Cassie twirled in front of the mirror and smiled. If she was sensible she'd add a plain white t-shirt and flip-flops. But on went a sleeveless white silky top and the cute blue kitten-heeled sandals she'd bought in a sale.

For her hair she compromised by drawing some back from her face and tied the curls in a thin blue ribbon, leaving the rest loose and wild. Nothing to do with her memories of Jay's enjoyment of her hair the only time they were together. Not at all.

Cassie ran downstairs and headed for the door, calling back over her shoulder, 'I'm off,' then disappeared before her mother could see her and make more nasty, pointed comments.

The short walk cooled her off, but

the first sight of Jay reignited the heat. His smile pierced through the crowd of people, zooming in on her. She sort-of floated across the room and he immediately stood, towering over her and bent to kiss her cheek. The fleeting warm touch and his lingering musky cologne brought memories flooding back.

'I've ordered you a Chardonnay — is that alright?'

Alcohol was a bad idea but she nodded anyway. Disagreeing would mean speaking and her mouth didn't appear to be working. Did he realise she couldn't drag her eyes off him?

His thick, dark hair, grown slightly too long would feel like heavy silk under her fingers. His tight black jeans showed every inch of his long, muscular legs and Cassie was pretty sure he'd had the shirt made to match his eyes, one moment blue, the next silvery gray.

They ate, although she couldn't have said afterwards what they'd had, and he kept the conversation light and friendly.

Disappointment snaked through her.

'How about taking our coffee outside?' Jay suggested and Cassie heard herself agree. 'Not too cool for you is it? I needed to get out of that crush.'

'It feels good to me.' The fresh air took the edge off her heated body but Jay took her hand and her face burned.

'You feel good. Extremely good.' His tempting voice slid over her skin, sending an exciting shiver down her spine.

She should tell him this wasn't right, that she couldn't do this again. But there were no false promises or misunderstandings, so maybe she'd handle it better this time?

Jay took his hand away and drank the last of his coffee, then put the cup back down and stared deep into her eyes.

'Cassie. I'm getting too old to play games. I'm desperate to make love to you and if I'm reading the signs right I think you want me to. Tell me straight out if I'm wrong and I'll be a complete, if frustrated, gentleman and take you home.'

She met his gaze head on.

'You're right. I can't stay late though or my parents will worry and that's the only thing I'm sorry for.'

His smile took away the last traces of apprehension in her.

Jay stood and held out his hand and Cassie took it. He pulled her up against him, so close she could barely breathe. One hand snaked up to her hair and untied the ribbon, running through her loosened curls. He trailed long, firm fingers down her neck and rubbed gently at where the tension lay.

He bent his head and his mouth molded to hers and she responded, losing herself in the taste and the power of him.

'We'd better go or I won't be able to stop,' Jay declared. No man ever wanted her this blatantly. 'Come on, you witch.'

'What a thing to call a good girl like me,' she teased.

He slid his hand down her spine and

cupped her backside, his growing arousal pressing into her belly. 'Please don't tell me you're a good girl, not now you've done this to me.'

Cassie's laugh brought out his glorious smile. 'I promise not to be at all good. Not that sort of good anyway.'

'Thank heavens.'

His exuberant kiss took away what remained of her doubt and Cassie hardly knew how they made it to Tony's house because her awareness only returned as Jay stood in front of her and began to very slowly to undress her, like a child opening a much yearned for Christmas present.

'Oh darlin' how did I get so lucky?'

'Because you asked really nicely.'

'I've always had good manners. My mo — .'

Suddenly he stumbled.

Cassie rested her hand against his cheek. 'What is it, Jay?'

'Nothing. I . . . come to bed.'

He eased away and quickly stripped off his own clothes, denying her the chance to take her time with him. Under the covers he wrapped himself around her so tightly his shivers became part of her.

'Why are you so cold?' she asked, puzzled.

'Warm me, Cassie. Just hold me. We'll talk later.'

His eyes shone with a frightening level of desperation and she succumbed, snaking her hand between them to caress his searing arousal, making him groan. His kisses trailed downwards until at last he took her breast in his mouth, licking and sucking until she reached almost fever pitch, then he gently pushed her hands to her sides and rubbed against her until she opened herself for him.

'Oh, Jay, please,' she begged, watching the passion flame in his eyes as his finger stroked and teased between her thighs, the fire there building almost unbearably.

'Is this what you want?' he breathed.

She clenched around his probing

fingers until she came hard, gasping and meeting his satisfied smile.

Jay pushed up on his knees and reached on the bedside table for the foil packet, his breathing shallow and rushed, but he never took his eyes from her.

With mind-blowing control he slowly slid into her inch by tortuous inch. As their hip bones touched he paused and she felt the delicious fullness as he reached up to stroke her hair, gazing longingly over her face. Cassie wrapped her legs around his hips and he moaned, starting a steady rhythm she matched.

'You're so beautiful, my Cassie . . . '

*My Cassie.* She wished it were true. Pushing the thought away she gave herself up to the moment and rushed towards the edge of her climax. He picked up the pace, sensing her need and, with one last thrust, pushed her into that magical spiral of excitement. He tensed in her arms, every muscle rigid as he gave in to his own release, clinging to her until his body stilled.

Jay lay heavy and comforting against her sweat-slicked skin, his end-of-day stubble rasping against her cheek, and drifted off to sleep like a little boy worn out by the pleasures of the day.

★ ★ ★

When he opened his eyes, before he remembered she was there, Cassie saw the raw pain he couldn't hide.

She snuggled closer. 'Tell me what's wrong, Jay.'

Jay sighed and played with the ends of her hair.

'I'm not a good man, Cassie. I'm a lousy son and brother. I didn't come here because I'm such a great friend to Tony either. I'm here because I couldn't be where I was any longer. My . . . my mother died and I'm not handling it well. Things are falling apart at work, too.'

'I'm sorry. When did she . . . ?'

'Nearly a month ago.'

The words sounded as if they'd been dragged from his throat. 'It was a typical night in Jay Burton's wonderful life.'

He tried to pull away but Cassie snaked her arms around him and held on tight.

'I purposely screwed another woman so my girlfriend would dump me and I didn't give a damn, so I got drunk and passed out. I woke up to a clutch of missed phone calls from my family. Ma had forbidden them to tell me she was ill, said I was too busy and didn't need to be worried. I went straight home and stayed a week but left after the funeral because I couldn't handle it. I ended up here because I hadn't a clue where else to go . . . ' He sighed again, as if he was completely spent. 'And there was you . . . ' His stormy eyes fixed on her. 'You wouldn't leave my mind and I had to find out what might . . . what could be. I've no clue what to do next, Cassie. I'm not good at long-term relationships.'

'Have you ever tried? Do you want to?' She held her breath.

How could a man think straight with this vision of loveliness leaning in over him? All smooth warm skin, golden hair and eyes dark as the midnight sky. Right now he'd say anything to keep her here. He didn't know her whole story yet but realised she didn't need him messing her around.

Jay heard her disappointed sigh and caught a glisten of tears in her bewitching eyes. He couldn't give her up. Not yet.

He cupped her face with his hands and kissed her deep pink lips, swollen with his loving. He'd say what she wanted to hear and hope he could live up to her expectations. His mother said he'd grow up one day and maybe this was his chance?

'Will you help me?' he whispered.

'Yes, but I'm scared too, Jay. Since you came back I've been determined not to get involved with you, not after Italy. I couldn't reply to your letter the

97

other day because I was too angry.'

'I deserve your condemnation, but I won't hurt you again. I've changed.' Jay wanted to believe it more than anything.

Her rueful smile said she'd like to believe him too, but couldn't. 'You can't promise, so don't.' Cassie's voice was barely a whisper.

Jay hated the fact she was right.

'Will you take me home now? If you're feeling brave you can come in and meet my parents.'

Worry lines crinkled her brow and Jay knew she already regretted asking. Should he refuse or rise to the challenge?

'I'd like that.' Liar. He slid his hands down to her slender waist and bent to touch his mouth to her rounded breast, so temptingly close. Cassie's moan undid him and he raised his eyes to her. 'But not for a few minutes, though. Please.'

Her smile was the answer he'd hoped for.

* * *

Jay held out his hand to Cassie's father and received a reluctant handshake in return. The man's sunken pale blue eyes briefly studied him then looked away. William Moore slumped back into the old brown leather chair and sunk back into silence.

Jay flashed his best smile at Barbara Moore but it fell on the proverbial stony ground. His outstretched hand was ignored and her dark, shrewd eyes stabbed him through the heart.

'So, Mr Burton, you're Irish,' she said as if accusing him of being an alien. There wasn't much he could do except nod. 'From a large family, are you?'

Jay wanted to defend his country and his family but tried not to offend the old woman, for Cassie's sake.

'I'm from a small village outside Dublin. I've three sisters and two brothers. My father's retired so Colum runs the family farm. Iona and Eamon are both teachers, Deidre's a hairdresser and Siobhan's a cook but she's just had her third baby so is busy with the little ones.'

'You didn't want to stay there too?'

'I wanted a different sort of life. I'm a banker in London.'

'Typical. Young people always want to leave. Think everything's better somewhere else,' she snipped.

'You're fortunate to still have Cassie with you,' Jay stated with a smile but Mrs Moore sniffed in disdain.

'Only because she got herself in trouble at sixteen. She's very lucky with how good we've been to her,' Mrs Moore declared with a self-righteous glare.

Cassie's face set in a rigid mask and Jay purposely took hold of her cold hand. *Her mother picked the wrong man to mess with,* Jay thought; she'd taken his smooth, handsome appearance to mean he was slick and useless. *Big mistake.*

'Cassie's obviously a good, loving

mother and she's amazing in the book shop too; all the customers love her. I'm sure she could do anything she put her mind to.' He spoke to Mrs Moore but his words were for Cassie.

'Good mother? The boy's a — '

'That's enough, Mother. Jay doesn't need the gruesome details, thank you very much.'

He did, but this wasn't the time. 'I'd better be going,' Jay said politely. 'I hope to see you again.'

Mrs Moore snorted. 'I shouldn't think it's likely. Cassie can't keep men long.' She turned away to watch the television game show her husband was already engrossed in.

Cassie practically dragged Jay to the door, her face flushed with anger and shame, where he pulled her into his arms and she let her head rest against his chest. He ran a hand up and down her spine in slow, languid strokes.

'It's OK, my darlin' girl. How about going out tomorrow afternoon? I'd offer to take you to lunch but I figure you'll be busy with the cheerful pair in the other room.'

His touch of humor brought a tentative smile to her face.

'Alright. Pick me up in your pretty car at two o'clock — and don't bring me back too soon.'

'I promise to keep you out until I've had my wicked way with you — several times.' He loved her raunchy laugh. 'Behave yourself 'til then.' He tweaked her nose and headed for his car.

Jay hated to drive off and leave Cassie there and his eyes fixed on the rear-view mirror as she stood on the doorstep and watched until he was out of sight.

*   *   *

Maybe he'd found the woman to match him at last. He'd suggested a walk and she'd willingly agreed, and now Jay was discovering the reason she had such great legs — Cassie could go for miles without flagging or complaining.

She'd love the Irish countryside.

He'd always turned down his mother's suggestions to bring his latest girlfriend home because none would have fitted in. It was scarily easy to picture Cassie with his family, laughing and listening to their stories.

She strode out in front of him, easily negotiating the rough ground, her hair in a loose ponytail, whipped around by the stiff breeze. Her hand gestured to the huge granite tor looming over to their right.

'Don't you love this?'

Who could help but respond to her? Had the men in her life been maniacs? Her face gleamed and with no make-up to hide behind every thought played out for him to see. Jay ran a few steps to catch up with her, swung her into his arms and pulled her close enough to smell pure, unadulterated woman. Her cool lips warmed in an instant and he couldn't resist plunging into their sweetness until he struggled to remember how to breathe.

'I was going to suggest we went in

somewhere for tea when we finish our walk but I've changed my mind.'

Cassie's eyes sparkled and her arms reached up and pulled him back to her mouth. Her searching kiss and the way her body rubbed against his made him wish they were anywhere but on an exposed moor with other walkers heading towards them.

'You're an evil woman, Cassie Moore.' He swatted her behind — not very gently. 'Get back to my car, now!'

'What'll happen if I don't?'

He told her very explicitly and watched her face flush with a flare of heat.

⋆ ⋆ ⋆

They sat outside her house like a couple of teenagers reluctant to end a date. The hour they'd sneaked at Tony's cottage only managed to dampen the edge of their passion, leaving them barely sated.

'You sure you want to come in after

last time?' Cassie asked with a questioning glance.

'I was brought up to always take a lady home, which meant all the way to her door,' Jay asserted.

Cassie moved away and Jay instantly felt the loss of her warmth. Her eyes resonated with sadness.

'I'd like to tell you more about . . . about Sam and everything but I'm not sure if I'm really ready share it just yet.'

Jay stroked his hand over the soft, wild curls hanging down her back. 'It's OK. When you're ready I'll listen, otherwise I'm fine. Come on, let's go in.'

'Cassandra Louise, is that you?'

Mrs Moore's sharp voice drifted into the hall the instant they stepped through the front door and anger flared inside Jay as Cassie's shoulders slumped.

'Yes, Mother.'

'Get in here. The police have been again.'

Jay touched her arm. 'You're busy. I'll . . . I'll see you at work tomorrow.'

Disappointment clouded Cassie's eyes. His intention was to not interfere in her personal business but he'd read it wrong. He often did that — disappointed people. Nevertheless, he headed for the door, knowing he should turn around.

*Go back and listen,* he told himself. *Really listen this time. Do something to help.* But he didn't.

Cassie briefly closed her eyes to gain strength from deep inside. Jay's retreating back made it clear she needn't bother looking in his direction. What had she expected?

'I won't be able to hold my head up in the street soon. What with you having that boy out of wedlock and now this. People will see the police cars outside our house day and night.'

'Don't exaggerate, Mother. Tell me what they said today.' Cassie sighed.

'They asked the same questions again. Didn't seem to believe me when I said we hadn't heard anything from Sam. The girl's father is kicking up a fuss saying they aren't doing enough to find her. Typical. They always blame the ones who've got no money to fight back. One of them wanted to poke around Sam's room again. I told him he could get a bloody warrant or get out of my house.'

Cassie stared in disbelief. Her mother was almost defending Sam — something she'd never done — and Cassie came close to smiling because Barbara Moore never swore, and only wished Sam could have heard his Gran.

Impulsively she hugged her mother and saw the flash of surprise. 'Thanks.'

'I'm not going to be spoken to that way. Give some people a badge and a title and they think they're God. Now get us some tea. I'm parched.'

Cassie knew not to push her luck.

* * *

A rainy day meant not many customers which equated to long hours being polite to Jay. They circled each other all morning and took separate lunch hours but there were still three hours to go until closing time.

'Coffee?' He held out her favorite extra-large, dark green mug, with *Book Diva* decorating it in extravagant gold letters, as a peace offering. 'You can drink it or throw it at me. You decide.'

Jay stood motionless, focusing hard on her from under heavy, sleep deprived eyes.

'You look more in need of it.' She refused to get any closer to softening.

'I have one too.' He brandished Tony's Shakespeare mug. 'Come and sit with me, please.'

He waited for her to choose a spot and sat as far away as the battered red sofa allowed.

'I should've . . . ' she started to explain.

'Cassie, please don't say anything until I've apologised properly. I've thought of nothing else since yesterday. I was a jerk. I don't care what you have or haven't told me, nothing excuses my behavior. My mother would be ashamed of me.' The words cracked in his throat.

'She'd be proud of you for putting it right now.' She guessed it might've been the first time he'd ever apologised to a woman.

'We didn't talk much when we first met did we?' Jay said with a wry smile.

She gently poked his arm. 'And whose fault was that?'

They both burst out laughing and suddenly it was alright. Jay swept her hands into his, squeezing tight. 'Can we start again?'

She nodded, extricated her hands and then holding out the right one for him to shake.

'Hello. I'm Cassie Moore. I'm thirty-two and I live in Cornwall with my parents. I'm a single mother to my sixteen-year-old son, Sam and I've never been married.'

The sparkle was back in his eyes, drawing her in inexorably.

'Patrick Jay Burton, Pat to my family

and Jay to everyone else. I'm thirty-eight, Irish with loads of brothers, sisters, nieces and nephews. I grew up near Dublin and after university became a banker in London. I've never been married either.'

'There, that got the potted versions out of the way, I suppose you need a few more specifics?' She couldn't leave him wondering any longer. 'I left school at sixteen because I was pregnant. Sam's father, Pete Wilson, left as soon as he found out about the baby and I never saw him again. As far as I know he's still in prison for drug dealing and assault. My parents took us in and, well, you know what they're like. I should be grateful but it's not easy. This job is the first one I've had. I guess I've screwed up the mothering thing but I . . . ' Her words trailed away as slow tears tracked their way down her cheeks.

Jay brushed them away with his thumbs and pressed a soft, warm kiss on her mouth.

'Children don't always turn out the way they're expected to. My family wanted different for me as well.'

'But you're very successful. Why wouldn't they be happy?'

His eyes clouded and he struggled to meet her gaze.

'They think my life's soulless and maybe they're right. An expensive flat, flashy car and designer clothes don't make a good person, do they?'

'No, but they don't make a bad one either. Living in an old house with your parents, travelling by bus, and wearing secondhand clothes don't make a great one either. It's what's in here that counts.' She rested her hand on his heart, feeling the steady beat through his shirt.

'How can you not realise what an amazingly smart woman you are?' Jay asked, his words vehement and sure.

'Can we try again?' Cassie ventured.

'We're making a habit of this, aren't we?'

They smiled and moved into each

other's arms and hugged warmly for a few moments.

'Good grief. Leave some people to run a shop and they turn it into a brothel. Take your hands off each other at once, children.' Tony's dramatic laughter filled the room.

'What're you doing back?' Cassie and Jay said in unison.

'Hell, they talk in tandem as well,' Tony joked.

Cassie stood, dropped her head slightly, and smiled up at her boss, deliberately fluttering her eyelashes. 'We've got everything straight out here and in the back and profits have gone up. Are we forgiven?'

'Only if you make me a cuppa before I collapse from exhaustion.'

'Of course, although I have to say for someone tired you look amazingly tanned and healthy.' Cassie proclaimed.

Tony hugged her. 'Flattery will get you everywhere.'

'Good to see the Aussies haven't changed you.' Jay joined in. 'Cassie, this man will say anything to get women throwing themselves at him, be warned.'

Tony winked and hugged Cassie tighter. 'Worked didn't it?'

'Yeah, like a charm, now take your hands off my woman.'

'*Your* woman?' Cassie and Tony said together, in shock.

Jay's face flushed red. 'I'll leave you two to laugh at me while I make the tea for a change.'

Cassie wanted to fill the silence but Tony only stared hard at her. Her heart raced as he wandered off to check out the shop. Was it only his approval of the changes they'd made that she wanted, or more?

'Are you happy?' Tony's sudden question took her aback.

'Happy?'

'Yeah. You know — the way people feel when things are going well in their life.' His voice thickened. 'I didn't think you'd fall for it again, Cassie.'

'Fall for what?'

'Jay's inch thick Irish charm.'

The edge of bitterness in his voice shocked her. 'I thought he was your friend?'

'What's that to do with anything? It doesn't mean I trust him with your heart.' Tony's piercing eyes cut through her. 'Don't worry. I understand you don't see me 'that way.' I'll never understand why women go for men who treat them badly. Surely you aren't all stupid enough to think you'll be the one to reform them? Jay's a decent man underneath but he's so determined not to be that you're wasting your time. A professional psychologist could spend months on him and get nowhere.'

Cassie struggled for a reply that wouldn't make things worse. 'I'm sorry, Tony. You're a dear friend but I didn't realise . . . '

'My problem is I'm too damn nice. I changed after my years in London and started treating women the way I'd want to be treated, but it's not been very successful. They see me as good old Tony, best friend and shoulder to

114

cry on. Don't worry I'll live — and I'll be here to pick up the pieces when he runs off again.'

'What if he doesn't this time?'

Tony gave a sarcastic snort. 'Oh, he will. Our Jay doesn't do long term. He's allergic to the word commitment.'

'Do you really think it's your place to say?' Jay interrupted, his voice throbbing with anger.

'Is it true?' Cassie hated her hard, plain words but she needed to know.

'Can we talk, on our own?' he asked with a sigh.

'It's not necessary. You've given me my answer and it's pretty much the one I expected.'

'Please, over dinner tonight? Be fair.'

Jay's quiet plea tore at her heart. Cassie nodded while wanting to smack herself around the head for being so stupid.

She would not end up in bed with Jay tonight. She wouldn't.

\* \* \*

With dinner finished Jay made his move. They'd kept the conversation light while they ate, seemingly by mutual consent, so it was time to push his luck. He took a room key out from his pocket and laid it on the table between them.

'Am I being presumptuous?'

A flush lit up Cassie's face. 'You got a room here just to . . . ?'

'No. I couldn't stay with Tony after what happened in the shop earlier. The fact it gives us privacy is a bonus.' *Flanneler.* His brother's mocking voce reverberated in his head. 'It's up to you. And if you just want to talk it's fine too, although it's already killing me to sit here and not touch you.'

Jay met her dark eyes straight on and didn't flinch.

'I wouldn't want to be responsible for your demise,' her sly smile aroused him in a second.

'I appreciate your concern.'

Jay stood and held out his hand, catching his breath when she placed hers trustingly inside. He didn't deserve her trust. If they weren't in public he'd sweep her into his arms and run upstairs with her before she came to her senses.

'We'll talk afterwards.' Cassie murmured and he lifted her hand to his lips, brushing a grateful kiss over her warm skin.

She didn't appear to mind him steering her from the bar and up to his room without speaking. Jay unlocked the door with trembling hands and pulled her inside, pushing her against the wall and seizing her mouth in a searing kiss. Her subtle perfume teased his senses and Jay lost all notion of taking it slow.

Cassie gasped as he shoved her skirt up out of the way, stroking her through her black lace panties. Her response to his touch made him grin.

'Glad we're on the same line of thought, darlin' girl.'

With his other hand Jay eased his zipper down and freed himself from his boxers. She glanced down and her appreciative smile brought an instant reaction, pressing his desire into her as she flung her head back and moaned, giving him better access to her neck. He kissed and nipped at her soft skin, wanting to mark her as his own.

For a second he considered moving to the bed but couldn't wait. He groped in his pocket for the foil packet and slid his arms around her back.

'Look at me, Cassie,' he growled softly, desperate to watch every expression on her beautiful face.

Jay thrust hard and impatiently, sinking into her welcoming depths, starting a pounding rhythm without waiting. He didn't need to, because she tightened and clenched around him and he knew she was close.

'Come with me.' Jay stroked his finger across her thighs and delved into her core, capturing her cry of pleasure in his mouth. As he pulled back from their deep kiss, the sight of her ecstasy tipped him over the edge and he jerked hard, giving in to his own release. As their bodies stilled he clung on tight for what felt like forever, struggling to hold them upright but afraid to move.

Jay buried his nose into her hair, a lose, shimmering mass of curls. 'You're amazing,' he said reverently and she sighed against his neck. Carefully he lowered her to the floor and eased himself from her body, pushing a strand of hair away from her face, the better to stare into her glazed eyes.

'How about we get undressed this time?'

'This time?' Her lilting question stirred him back to life and he took her hand and placed it on him, smiling into her laughing eyes as he swelled into the power of her touch.

'Alright. If you insist.'

'I do.'

Later, wrapped around her lush body, boneless with loving her, Jay wanted to push away everything but the here and now.

'You're going back to London aren't

you?' Cassie said in a steady voice. 'You can hardly stay now Tony's back and you're too scared of anything long-term with me, aren't you?'

'How about you come home with me for a few days?' He avoided answering outright. 'I'll show you what my car can really do.' He dropped a kiss on the back of her neck, making her shiver. 'We'd have the weekend to ourselves. You'll love the wharf, there are gorgeous shops, amazing restaurants and the view from my flat is something else.'

Cassie pulled out of his arms and slid off of the bed.

'Grow up, Jay. I'm not stupid enough to believe this can work and you aren't either.' Her eyes turned the cold blue of a winter sea. 'I don't belong in your fancy bankers' world. My Oxfam renovated clothes would hardly impress your friends. Go back to your glossy women. They won't ask too much of you, which I'm sure suits you perfectly.'

He respected her enough not to lie again.

Cassie picked up a blue silky robe from the chair and slid in on over her tempting curves, cinching the belt tightly. 'I'm going to have a shower then I'll walk home.'

'There's no need . . . '

'Yes, there is a need, Jay. I'm a capable woman who doesn't have to be babied. We don't all have the luxury of indulging our selfish desires anytime we want. I've got a mother who needs help bathing and a father who wants his hot cocoa made the right way before bed. I have responsibilities even if you don't.'

Jay bit his lip, but didn't say a word, only watched her go.

# 6

Let the police stop him! Jay slammed the accelerator to the floor and shifted into fifth gear. A couple of hundred miles of full-throttle driving might sort out his screwed up head.

He'd received a text from Paul and the rest of the gang from work to say they'd be in the Blue Room at nine tonight. He'd have a few drinks and catch up on the office gossip to get back in the swing. On Monday it'd be work as usual.

Three hours and twenty minutes. Jay swung into the garage with a grin on his face. He leapt out of the car and threw his keys at Brian.

'We missed you, Mr Burton.'

Jay tapped the gleaming car and chuckled. 'No, you haven't, you've only missed this little baby, admit it.'

Laughter lines creased Brian's face as

he struggled not to smile. 'She's a pretty one, I must say.'

'I'll grab my bags and you can park her for me. Fill her up before tomorrow, will you and put it on my account?'

'Certainly, sir. You're not going out tonight, Mr Burton?'

'Yes, but I'm walking. I'd never risk this beauty when I'm drinking.'

'Planning on indulging, are you, sir?'

Jay's face darkened. 'Oh yeah. Seriously. It's time I got reacquainted with some good Irish whiskey. I've been good for far too long.'

*  *  *

Jay knocked back another whiskey and glanced around him. This was a wildly successful evening by the standards he'd set before coming out. He was back in the loop about who'd hit on some big trades and who was struggling, drunk enough to sink the QEII and now the much sought after Livvy

123

Robson-Pierce — tall, blonde and hot enough to set a man on fire — was draped over him. The woman had serious brains; last year she'd made more money than any of the men, and she was extremely particular whose bed she'd grace with her presence. The way she stroked his thigh made it clear he was tonight's lucky victim.

Jay pulled her head roughly to him and plundered her mouth and her taste and smell startled him — a combination of Grey Goose Vodka and Chanel instead of Cassie's innocent toothpaste and magnolia. He slid one hand up her tight black skirt and she writhed against his fingers.

'My place. Now,' he growled and she gave a satisfied smile.

An hour later Jay lay back in his bed and studied Livvy, stark naked and smoking a cigarette out on the balcony, uncaring whether anyone watched.

'It happens to all men, Jay, although I must admit hadn't expected it of you,' she said through the partly open balcony door. Her voice was forced as she tried to put on a sympatheitc veneer, but it was plain she was irritated. 'I'd heard very good reports about your . . . performance.'

Stubbing the cigarette out in her vodka glass she casually pulled her clothes back on, covering her rail thin body.

What'd been appealing in the alcohol induced fog of the Blue Room turned cold and sordid in his bedroom. She'd tried every trick in the book, including a few he'd never experienced before, but nothing had worked.

All he wanted was for her to be gone. He ached for a hot shower and sleep — if only Cassie's disgusted face would leave his brain alone. He had the idea she wouldn't, and was sure he deserved her contempt, too.

⋆ ⋆ ⋆

'Come on, Cassie, it'll do you good. Take pity on this lonely old bachelor.

Soon I'll be getting a tabby cat and a brown cardigan with suede patches on the elbows.'

Tony's fake sadness made her smile. She hadn't been out for months, not since Jay left, so what was wrong with accepting his invitation?

'Thanks, it'll make a nice change. Would Saturday be alright? I'll ask Mary Tremayne to sit with Mum and Dad for the evening.'

'Perfect. Put your prettiest dress on and we'll go dancing.' Tony declared with a wide smile.

'Dancing? I thought you meant a drink or dinner.'

'You like to dance, don't you?' Tony asked.

'Well, yes, I suppose so but the last time I went they were still playing Madonna and the Pet Shop Boys.' Cassie purposely smiled, not wanting Tony to feel sorry for her pitiful social life.

'There's a nice club in Falmouth that caters to people who like good music and good conversation without it being spoiled by hordes of drunken teenagers.' Cassie winced and a rush of heat lit up Tony's face. 'I'm so sorry. I didn't mean . . . '

'I know. You'd never deliberately hurt anyone and that's a rare thing. The club sounds lovely.'

For a moment he held her gaze with his bright green eyes and a tingle of anticipation stirred in the base of her stomach.

★　★　★

'I'm just going up to change, Mum.' Cassie stood and headed for the stairs.

'Not a tarty outfit. You know men can't be trusted.'

'Tony's a good friend, that's all,' she defended him.

'Don't be stupid, Cassandra. Men are never 'friends' with women. They're all after one thing and knowing you, you'll be stupid enough to give it out. I notice we don't see anything of the no good Irishman anymore. He didn't last long, did he?'

Cassie didn't know whether to laugh or cry. No wonder her self-esteem was battered when her own mother held such a low an opinion of her.

She'd have a good evening out and maybe allow Tony to kiss her goodnight. Maybe.

All too soon Tony picked her up and the drive to Falmouth passed in their normal, easy conversation. Cassie pushed aside the fact this was a sort-of date, not a day at work.

The choice whether to go in a different direction came before she was ready. The slow dance happened out of the blue. One minute they were happily bopping to a 70s disco number and the next Tony slid his arms around her waist and her head rested naturally against on his chest as he swayed her gently to the rhythym. Her teenage boyfriends had never managed more than lumbering around the dance floor a few times to keep her happy so they'd get what they wanted at the end of the evening.

'You didn't tell me you could dance.' Cassie half-protested.

'You didn't ask. We had all kinds of dance classes in drama school. Another day I'll put on my tap shoes and really impress you if you're very lucky.'

'Is there no end to your talents?' she teased and Tony gave her a strangely searching look. He moved closer and as his body pressed against hers Cassie became aware of the effect she was having on him.

Tony touched his warm lips to hers, just one notch up from friendly. 'Are you ready to go?'

Under the strobe lights his eyes shimmered with desire and for a second she faltered. Suddenly he smiled and returned to everyday Tony again.

'Come on, Cinderella.'

Outside the chill, night air shook her brain back into place. A few minutes ago, wrapped in his arms with hypnotic music throbbing around them, it had seemed possible. Why couldn't she love him the way he wanted her to? Tony was good looking, kind, intelligent and interested. What was wrong with her?

His ancient Ford Escort struggled to life but Tony made no effort to drive off and let the engine die back to silence.

'It's alright, Cassie.'

She met his eyes, so full of genuine caring and squeezed his hand. 'I'm sorry, Tony, I really am. I wish . . . '

'Me too, but your wishes are different from mine and that's the way it is. Please don't stop being my dear friend though.'

He ran one finger lightly down the side of her face and tears burned in her eyes.

'Don't cry, please. I don't ever want to make you cry. I'll take you home and give you our regular, friendly kiss on the cheek. In the morning we'll work as usual and everything will be as it was.' They were brave words but he couldn't quite look at her. 'Of course all my saintly talk doesn't mean that if Jay was

130

here I wouldn't smash his pretty face in.'

They both laughed but he turned away from her.

\* \* \*

After he left she sat alone in the darkened house.

Where was Sam sleeping tonight? Were he and Lindy under a bridge with a crowd of dirty homeless drunkards or in a filthy squat packed with drug takers? Maybe Lindy had money? Cassie would bet anything she had her own credit card backed up by a healthy bank account. Would she dare use it when her father might check on her?

If Sam came home things would have to change. She'd lay down rules and he'd obey them. He'd go back to school or get a job and help around the house. There'd be no going out drinking. Cassie laughed sadly to herself. The idea of Sam obeying any of her crazy rules after going his own way for so long was ridiculous. But she'd seen the desperate look in his eyes. Deep down Cassie guessed he wanted her to stand up to him, needed her to be in charge and wanted to be nothing more than a normal mixed-up teenager.

Maybe it was time to tell Sam about his father? For years Sam asked about him continually, only stopping when she wouldn't give any answers beyond his name and the fact he'd left them and was now in prison. Perhaps he needed more knowledge to grow up; after all everyone craved the security of where they came from good or bad.

She'd slept with Pete's photo under her pillow until the day Sam was born but when she cradled the downy head of her new born son she packed it away. The single photo she had of Sam's raven haired father straddling his motorbike, all black leather, tattoos and arrogance, was buried in the back of her wardrobe. Once a year, on Sam's birthday, she'd taken it out until the day she heard he'd been sent to prison for drug dealing. It'd spent the last seven years in a sealed box.

Cassie quickly snatched the ringing phone so it wouldn't wake her parents.

'Mum?'

Her heart missed a beat.

'Sam? Where are you? Are you alright? Silence. 'Sam, please. Just tell me you're OK.'

His voice sounded gruff and unused. 'Yeah. I'm fine. Lindy's here, too.'

Cassie barely held onto her patience. 'Where's here, Sam?'

'She told me not to . . . '

'Sam. Tell me right now where you are. It was wrong of you to leave that way and Lindy's parents are frantic. They've got the police looking for you both.'

'But we're sixteen and — '

'Sam, it doesn't matter how old you are when you know the right people. If you stay away you'll be in big trouble.'

'She won't come home, Mum . . . ' Sam's voice cracked. 'I want to but she likes London.'

'Where are you?' Cassie shouted, not caring who heard.

'We're in Hackney. Stoke Newington. Russell Road — '

The phone went dead and Cassie held the empty receiver for a very long time before gently hanging up. Immediately she dialed Tony's number. She couldn't abandon her work and there were things to arrange here, but by lunchtime tomorrow she'd be on the train to London. She would bring Sam home.

\* \* \*

'Not waking you am I, mate?'

Jay glanced at the clock and chuckled at Tony's question. Only midnight. Since he got back from Cornwall he'd existed on a couple of hours sleep a night, barely eating and working all the hours his brain could keep functioning. He'd never made as much money in such a short time. His boss was thrilled.

'Hardly. How're you doin'?'

134

Tony hesitated. 'I'm OK, but . . . '

'Is something wrong with Cassie?'

'She's fine but she needs your help and is too stubborn to ask. She'll cut my balls off when she finds out I've called you.'

'Spill it, Tony. What can I do and how do I do it without it resulting in your mutilation?' Jay teased and the humor brought their friendship back to close to normal.

'Sam called a short while ago and said he's in Stoke Newington with Lindy. He sounded scared and hung up quickly. The girl doesn't want to come back and Cassie thinks she stopped Sam from calling before. Cassie's getting the train up tomorrow but she doesn't know London, Jay. She wouldn't let me come with her and I'm worried she'll get into something she can't deal with.'

Jay's heart thumped wildly. 'What train is she getting?'

'It gets into Paddington at quarter past four.'

135

'Don't you worry. By the time she gets back to you I'll make sure she's taken out her anger on me — it shouldn't be difficult.'

'You aren't as bad as you make out, you know.'

'Yes I am Tony, you just never believed it.'

Jay quickly ended the conversation and went back to his computer screen, Sleep would certainly elude him tonight when all his mind saw was Cassie. He was being given another chance and he'd better not screw it up. Again.

★ ★ ★

He'd recognise Cassie's hair anywhere, a mass of shining gold in the middle of a sea of ordinariness. The second she spotted him her face flamed with anger and confusion.

'Hey, darlin' girl, good journey?' Jay beamed one of his best women-charming smiles.

She'd run away or turn her back on

him if it was possible, but stuck in the middle of a mass of people and carrying two bags there wasn't much she could do.

'What the devil are you doing here? Don't tell me, Saint Tony decided I needed a knight in shining armour?'

Jay snatched her luggage and dared to drop a kiss on her cheek. 'Now, be nice. I'm taking you to my place and you can tell me where Lindy and Sam might be and we'll plan it from there.'

'I haven't come to socialise. I'll be searching straightaway.'

'Hauling that lot as you go?' Jay pointed to her bags. She sunk into a mutinous silence. 'The car park's this way. A couple of minutes and we'll be on our way out of this crowd.'

She trailed beside him, a stony expression fixed firmly in place while he chattered on.

Unscathed. Jay always gave thanks when his beautiful car survived being parked in unsavory places.

'The traffic's not too bad today. We'll

be there in about twenty minutes if we're lucky.'

She pretended to watch where they were going but he caught her checking him out a couple of times. Good. He'd taken care in deciding what to wear and the effort had been worthwhile.

'Have you ever been to the Wharf before?' Cassie shook her head. 'This is the Icon. My place is at the very top,' he gestured in front of them and her eyes wandered all the way up the impressive ultra-modern building. Jay remembered the first day he'd seen it and truly believed he'd made it in life.

As he pulled into the parking garage Brian popped out from his office, wearing a broad and welcoming smile.

'We get out here, Cassie. We have to leave this darlin' with her keeper. He'll clean her and talk sweetly to her and if I'm lucky he'll let me take her out again later.'

'Mr Burton, shame on you. You're making fun of me, and in front of a lovely young lady too.' Brian tipped his hat to Cassie. 'I wouldn't trust him if I were you, Miss.'

Cassie laughed freely for the first time. 'Don't worry, I don't, not one inch.'

Jay cringed at the well-deserved, but unfortunate truth and took her elbow, steering her towards the glass enclosed lift.

'You'll love the view going up if you're not bothered by heights.' He pressed the button for the top floor and on the way he watched her eyes drink it all in before turning away, suspecting she felt guilty for enjoying it too much.

'Thankfully my cleaner's been in today,' he said as he opened the door. 'That's why it's so tidy. I'm naturally a bit of a slob, I'm afraid.'

She couldn't hide her stunned reaction and stared around at the pure white walls, huge black leather sofas, steel and glass, everything sharp and edgy and chosen by a top decorator purely to impress.

'Come see the view from the

balcony.' He edged her outside and placed his hand in the hollow at the base of her spine, pointing out the landmarks and feeling her tremble against his palm. 'How about some tea while you tell me what's going on?'

He must back off and be nothing more than a friend. For now.

Cassie's eyes sparkled in a direct challenge. 'Don't tell me you have ordinary tea in a place like this. Do you have to call the maid to bring it?'

'Faith and begorrah, surely you're not thinkin' a good Irish lad can exist without tea thick enough to stand a spoon up in, are you, me darlin'?'

The heavy overdone accent brought a reluctant smile to her lips, exactly as he'd hoped.

'You're hopeless, Jay Burton or should I call you Paddy?'

'My family all call me Pat, so you aren't far off.'

'Why Jay then?'

'It's my middle name. When I left Dublin I left Pat behind.'

'Can you do that?' she murmured and her deep blue eyes fixed on him, hard and curious.

Jay took her hand, expecting to be slapped away and gently stroked down her fingers as they lay compliantly in his. 'No. You can fool yourself for a while, but no — in the end you can't.'

An uneasy silence surrounded them despite the bustle of life going on twenty floors below.

Jay forced himself back to awareness. 'Come on. Tea and planning time.'

Her plight returned to her with a vengeance and the light left her face while he went to make tea.

Cassie wrapped her hands around the warm mug for comfort.

'Sam phoned and said he's alright so that's . . . ' The words choked in her throat.

'Where did he say he was?' Jay asked.

'Hackney, wherever that is.'

'Was he more specific?' Jay probed. 'It's a big area, love.'

'He said Stoke Newington, Russell

141

Road, but we were cut off before he said a number. I think Lindy made him hang up.'

'It's not the best area in London and isn't the sort of place where they'll take kindly to us asking too many questions. We'd better go in daylight, first thing in the morning, OK?'

'Alright. I'll meet you here, say around nine?'

His face darkened. 'Where are you planning to stay tonight?'

Cassie's chin lifted. 'I have some money. I'll find a hotel.'

'Oh no, you won't. You're not wandering around by yourself and don't argue. I have two guest bedrooms so you don't have to worry about being pounced on.'

She heard the unspoken, 'unless you want to be' and her face heated.

'Why don't you freshen up and we'll go out for dinner?'

'That's very kind but I don't have anything dressy to change into.' She might as well be honest, something they

142

weren't expert at between them.

'Don't worry. We'll go somewhere casual.'

Cassie glanced out the window. Nothing looked casual to her eyes out there.

'It's just food.' Jay said firmly.

She turned away to head for the bathroom, needing to get away from his overwhelming presence for a few minutes so she could steady herself.

⋆ ⋆ ⋆

Her mother would say Cassie had no place here.

When Jay rattled off a list of restaurants she latched onto the Cafe Rouge because he'd described it as, 'Parisian bistro meets London's East End.'

But there wasn't much sign of the East End as she glanced around at the other glamorous diners, eating their gourmet food and swilling bottles of fine wine — a world away from the people who'd once worked here.

'Hard to believe it was the busiest dock in the world once, isn't it?' Jay broke into her musings.

'Sad really.'

'Life changes and we've got to change with it. You can't go back,' he stated very plainly.

'Never?' She wasn't talking about the docks anymore and waited for his reply.

Jay shrugged. With his long legs stretched out in front of him, a glass of merlot in one hand and idly breaking off pieces of crusty baguette with the other, he fitted in perfectly — on the surface. It made her wonder where he fitted in deep down underneath, if anywhere.

'Where're we going to start tomorrow?' Cassie struggled to keep her focus on why she was here.

'I spoke with Brian while you were getting ready. Stoke Newington's a rough area so we've done a deal and I'm borrowing his car, in return he gets to take his wife out in the BMW on her birthday. He's given me his brother-in-law's phone number, he lives over that way and offered to come along.'

'That's good of him,' Cassie swallowed her pride, 'And you too. Why are you doing this for me?' His intense gaze skewered her and she changed her mind. 'Don't answer.'

Jay's mysterious twist of a smile made her shiver. She'd landed herself in big trouble now.

# 7

Cassie knew she wouldn't survive this unscathed. It'd been bad enough walking back from dinner with his hand swinging by his side, inches away from hers, but never quite touching.

Now they sat on separate sofas with a tray of coffee on the massive glass and stainless steel table between them. She guessed the elegant black and white china cost more than the whole contents of her kitchen back home.

He stared over to the window, rigid tension evident in every muscle of his body, his bare feet tapping on the thick white rug.

'It's been a long day. Do you mind if I have a bath and go on to bed?'

Jay flashed a tight smile. 'I'll get some clean towels for you.' He jumped up and strode out into the hall.

The oversized, rich red towels he

thrust into her hands were incredibly soft, nothing like the worn out ones she used.

Cassie usually enjoyed the rare opportunity to linger in a hot, perfumed bath but tonight her body wouldn't relax.

After a few minutes she climbed out of the massive tub and dried off. An elegant black wicker basket on the marble countertop contained an incredible selection of toiletries, no doubt intended for the sophisticated women he normally entertained. Cassie selected a tall bottle of lotion and poured some into her hand. A potent smell filled the air and she decided gold would smell this way if it had an aroma, rich and sumptuous. Cassie rubbed slowly, the strokes of her fingers soothing her overheated skin.

It was almost sacrilegious to put on the old pink t-shirt she'd brought to sleep in but she had no choice. Although it reached her knees she kept her sensible white panties on in some kind of crazy form of protection. She'd leave the bathroom, say a quick goodnight to Jay and escape to her bedroom. It wasn't so much that she didn't trust him. It was herself she didn't trust.

Poised at the corner of the hallway she called over to Jay and prepared to flee. 'See you in the morning!'

He swiveled around from staring out of the window and his eyes swept over her, burning a fiery liquid silver. She tugged on the hem of her nightdress.

'Come here, Cassie.' His low, molten words turned her into a puddle of unwanted desire and almost in a trance she crossed the room, stopping inches away from him.

Jay's right hand reached out, slid around her back and jerked her up against him. He fisted a handful of her loose curls and bent his mouth to hers. The deep, long kiss he took her into sucked out every sane brain cell she possessed. Through her thin t-shirt every rock hard inch of him rubbed

148

against her and almost unwillingly she pressed herself into his heat.

His hands slid up her thighs and with one swift move her nightdress was off and Cassie was lost, just as a frantic beeping noise filled the room.

'Damn.'

Jay cursed under his breath and his warm hands left her skin and groped in his pocket to pull out his phone. 'Yeah . . . when? Anchor Hospital? OK. We'll get right over there. Thanks. Tony.'

Jay gently slipped the t-shirt back over Cassie's trembling shoulders and pulled it down. He gave her a single gentle kiss, his eyes hazy with regret.

'That was Tony. Your father rang him because your mobile was turned off. Sam phoned home in a panic because Lindy's in the hospital. It's some sort of drug thing gone wrong from what Sam said. Get dressed quickly and we'll go.'

'Are you sure?'

'You think I'm going to insist on having my way with you first? What sort of man do you think I am?' His instant fury shamed her and Cassie rested her hand on his cheek.

'You misunderstood. I meant I could go by myself.'

'And my question's the same. Do you think I'd let you go alone?' He stood glaring, hands on hips.

'Don't do this to me, Jay, not now.' Tears seeped from her eyes and he softened, pulling her into a comforting embrace.

'I'm sorry. I overreacted, I don't mean to keep screwing us up,' he murmured into her hair.

'I know. Let me get ready and we'll leave.'

\* \* \*

'I hope your car will be OK here.' Cassie glanced around the crowded car park as they drove in to the hospital.

'It's a car. It's not a person I love. It's a chunk of metal. Pretty metal I'll agree, but that's all it is.' Jay replied,

150

almost surprising himself, but knowing it was true nonetheless.

Jay stopped by the front door of the hospital. 'I'll park and come in to find you. Off you go.' He cupped her face and gently kissed her before letting go with a reassuring smile.

Cassie made her way in, asking at the desk for the way to the Casualty department. She spotted Sam as she opened the door and her heart clenched in pain. How he'd aged in just these few short months. His shaved head was now inch long stubble and most of the piercings were gone and his badly washed black clothes had a stale gray sheen.

Sam turned and immediately stood up as she ran across the waiting room. A wave of relief crossed his face mixed with reassurance he wasn't alone. For the first time in years he voluntarily submitted to a hug and even hugged her back, gripping so tightly she was afraid to breathe.

'It's going to be OK. I'm here. We'll

make it right.' Cassie hoped she could follow through. It wouldn't be for lack of effort on her part.

'I told her not to take the stuff.' Sam choked back a sob.

'What happened?'

'We were at the pub and she bought some E off a dude. Said it'd be fun and she'd done it before. We went back to the place we're staying. She offered me one but I didn't take it and she laughed and called me a coward. Lindy took one with her rum and Coke. She got all happy and laughing, throwing herself at me, taking her clothes off and . . . '

A rush of heat colored his face and neck.

'Then she started shaking and her eyes went funny. I got her over to the bed and she passed out. I thought she'd be OK after she slept so I went to make coffee but when I got back she was moaning and twitching and her skin was bright red and sweating. I was frightened, Mum, I . . . '

Cassie captured his shaking hands in hers. 'You got her help. That was the right thing to do.'

'But I should have stopped her taking it in the first place. She could die.' Anguish filled his voice and she ached to take away his pain.

Jay strode into the waiting room and Sam pulled back and glared. 'Who the hell's he?'

'This is Jay Burton. He's a friend of mine. He was going to help me search for you both.'

'Oh yeah and what's he getting out of it? Thinks he's having you, does he? Or has he already?'

Cassie cringed. 'Please don't speak that way, Sam. Jay's been very kind.'

'I'll wait outside. Call me when you want to go back.'

Sam forced his angry face right into Jay's. 'Back where? She ain't stayin' with you!'

Jay took a step back and met Cassie's gaze. 'I'd rather stay to support you, but if you'd prefer me to leave.'

'Stay. Please.' Cassie pleaded, needing his comfort. He nodded and led her to sit down, his arm lightly draped around her shoulder, enough to comfort without being intrusive.

Sam glared at them both and put on the same sulky face he'd used since he was two and didn't get his own way.

★ ★ ★

Jay fingered Cassie's hair as she slept with her head on his shoulder. He should mind his own business but she deserved better. Someone had to speak up and Jay of all people only wished someone would urge Sam to be kinder to his own mother before it was too late.

'She's a good mother to you, Sam.'

'Mind your own bloody business.' The boy's face tightened and he flexed his hands, cracking his knuckles. Sam itched to hit him but couldn't do it here, though if Jay carried on seeing Cassie it would probably happen one day.

Jay almost made a snappy comeback but remembered being sixteen and at odds with the world. He watched his brothers and sisters get jobs locally, date and marry people they'd known since they were at school. He knew it wasn't for him, without having a clue what he wanted instead. Then he discovered the joy of making money and thought he'd found his place.

A young doctor entered the waiting room.

'Sam? Lindy's doing a little better. We contacted her parents earlier and they're on the way. I'm sorry but we're obliged to report any drug related incidents to the police. Somebody will be by tomorrow to ask you some questions I'm sure. You might as well go home now and get some rest.'

Sam sat upright and fixed a fierce glare on the doctor. 'I'm not going nowhere. I want to see her then I'll sleep here. You can't stop me.'

A faint trace of a smile pulled at the doctor's tired face. 'I wouldn't try, Sam.

You can come and see Lindy for a couple of minutes now if you'd like.'

Sam glanced warily at Jay who picked up on his uncertainty.

'It's alright. We'll be here waiting when you're done.'

Jay rested back in the chair and passed the time wondering how grim it was possible to make a room. Posters of contagious diseases were pinned crookedly on sickly green walls and hard black plastic chairs, curved at the wrong angles to ever get comfortable in made his back ache. A pile of scruffy old magazines lay in a pile on the table obviously well-thumbed by nervous people.

After fifteen minutes Sam ambled back in, the strain and exhaustion of the day pulling at his grey-tinged skin.

'Get some rest. They'll wake us if there's any news,' Jay encouraged him and Sam stretched out in the other corner, draping his thin body over several chairs.

'You could take Mum off to sleep proper if you want,' Sam threw the comment casually but Jay admired him for the first time. Lindy was wrong, the boy wasn't a coward.

'It's alright. We came to be with you so we'll stay.'

'Why're you doin' this?'

Cassie had asked the same question but Sam wouldn't be palmed off with the same noncommittal answer.

'I care about your mother. She was worried out of her mind about you and this was something I could do to help.' About as close to the truth as Jay could admit for now.

Sam shrugged and closed his eyes and a minute later Jay heard him quietly snoring and relaxed himself.

\* \* \*

'Where's the little bastard?' An overweight, balding man threw open the door and leapt across the room. 'What'd you do to my daughter?' He grabbed Sam by the throat and the boy flailed and gasped for breath.

157

Jay jumped up and none too gently dragged the stranger off Sam. 'Are you alright, kid?'

'What's going on ... ?' Cassie struggled awake and Jay went to her. 'Lindy's parents are here.'

'Get the police and lock this maniac up — and the murdering kid,' he yelled to his wife.

The doctor came in and stepped between them. 'Stop this now. Sit down and calm yourselves — both of you.'

Cassie pulled at Jay's arm and got him to sit down but adrenaline still coursed through his body and he took several deep, calming breaths.

'Thanks, mate.' Sam rubbed at his throat. 'He would've killed me.'

'What happened?' Cassie asked with a frown.

'Lindy's father's not too happy with Sam. He's obviously heard a different version of what actually happened.' Jay explained quietly.

'Hey, I'm telling the truth!' Sam said, outraged.

Jay touched the boy's shoulder. 'I didn't say you weren't. I believe you.' Oddly enough he did.

'Excuse me. I'm Amanda Retallick. Lindy's mother. You are?'

Jay hadn't realised she was in the room. He made introductions but no-one shook hands.

'I'm sorry about Peter. He's very upset about Lindy. Well, we both are but he . . . ' Her thin voice trailed away.

'The doctor said she was doing better?' Cassie ventured a tentative question.

'Yes. Luckily your son got her here quickly. They've cleared the worst of the drug from her system and they're rehydrating her while keeping an eye on her blood pressure and heart rate, they were both dangerously high but they're coming down.'

'I didn't buy the stuff or give it to her, Mrs Retallick.' Sam spoke up.

'I think we'll leave that to the police to check on, dear,' she said, not unkindly.

'I'm not talking to no bloody coppers.' Sam took off and sprinted from the room, crashing through the door and letting it slam shut behind him.

Jay stopped Cassie going after him. 'I'll go. Call my mobile if you hear anything. I'll keep him out of the way for a while.'

\* \* \*

A few enquiries led Jay out through a store room to a propped open door to the outside. Sam slumped on a low wall, a lit cigarette burning away in his fingers. Sam startled. 'Is Lindy . . .'

'There's no more news. Your mother's worried about you.'

Sam crushed the cigarette under the heel of his heavy black combat boots.

'Hospital are scary, aren't they?' Jay asked not expecting an answer and the boy stared down at his feet.

'What if she dies?' Sam glanced back up. 'They'll say it's my fault.' A single tear inched down his pale, drawn skin.

'I'm no expert but it sounds as though she'll be OK.' Jay tried to sound reassuring and Sam's shoulders dropped slightly.

'What if the police still charge me with something?'

'If the police take you in for questioning don't say anything, understand? I'll get you a lawyer if needs be.' Jay promised.

'Why?'

'I don't care to see anyone stamped on because they haven't got money and don't know the 'right' people. You ready to come back in?'

'I guess. You staying?' His dark black eyes bored into Jay.

'Yes, Sam, I'm staying.' Jay wasn't entirely sure what he'd promised but crossed his fingers he wouldn't let the boy — or Cassie — down. Not this time.

They headed back in and Jay steered Sam back into the waiting room while he went to search for coffee. He tackled

Lindy's doctor by the vending machine.

'You got any problem with me taking Sam and his mother home to my place? You can give the police my details if they want to contact us. I want the boy out of here in case Lindy's father has another go at him.'

The doctor stirred the murky liquid, staring into it as though he wished it was anything but disgusting hospital coffee.

'Fine. The girl needs to rest anyway. Come back later, maybe early evening, and she should be able to talk a little by then. That'll reassure Sam.'

\* \* \*

'You're kidding me, right?' Sam stared open-mouthed at the gleaming black convertible.

'You want to ride in the front and we'll let your mother squash into the back seat?'

Jay caught Cassie's approving smile as Sam leapt in immediately and his fingers trailed over the soft brown leather, lingering on the glossy walnut trim. '5 liter V-10 engine, right?'

'Yeah, she's a beauty isn't she?'

Sam nodded, envy burning from every pore. Jay understood only too well. One of the senior bankers gave him a lift in one of these when he was only low-ranking pond scum and it'd fired him up to tolerate anything they could throw at him. Childish maybe, but he still remembered how good it'd felt the day he got the keys in his hot hands.

'I can't really show you what she does on these roads but I'll take you out one day and we'll have some fun with her. If you want to.' Jay didn't expect an answer but Sam's flushed face was good enough.

Back at the Wharf he pulled into the garage and hopped out of the car. 'Sam, this is Mr Woods. He takes care of my car so I have to be nice to him.'

'Don't you listen to Mr Burton. He's Irish and they're great ones for teasing,'

Brian assured him and took hold of the keys.

By the time Jay opened the penthouse door Sam was struck dumb. The boy cautiously stepped inside and stopped dead on his heels. 'Hell.'

'It's not like where I grew up either,' Jay said.

'Didn't stay there though, did you?'

Jay turned away from the boy's piercing stare.

'Why don't you try and get some rest, Sam? You can have the room down on the left, it's got its own bathroom so you should find everything you need. Your mother's room is across the hall next to mine.'

He let out a breath he didn't realise he'd been holding as Sam shrugged and wandered off.

\* \* \*

'So, my darlin', what're we going to do to pass the time?'

Jay chuckled and pulled Cassie into

164

his arms, stroking his hands down her spine and making her shiver. Cassie reached up and ran her hands through his thick, silky hair.

'If Sam wasn't here I'd ask you to take me to bed and make me forget all of this mess.'

'My bedroom door has a lock, and you can sleep in your own room after. I'm sure he's dead to the world by now. Come on.' He cradled her face, pressing kisses into her warm skin and murmured sweet Irish nonsense, melting her completely.

On the threshold of his room Cassie stopped and stared.

'The decorator called it bachelor chic.' Jay's mocking tone made her smile. 'I thought the mirrored ceiling was a bit much but what does an Irish farm boy know about these things?'

His hands circled her hips and tugged at the hem of her t-shirt. 'You want to come and play, beautiful lady?' Jay yanked her into the room with a low, rumbling chuckle and reached

165

back to push the lock firmly into place. 'I recommend no screaming tonight though,' he joked.

'I've never been able to resist your smooth talk.'

He peeled off her top, then with one flick of his fingers her plain white bra was also consigned to the plush carpet.

'Thankfully, no.'

He flashed a wicked grin and swept her up into his arms and deposited her in the middle of the massive bed. Cassie sunk into the sumptuous white covers and he swiftly pulled off her shoes, skirt and panties.

'Taking your time tonight, are you?' she teased and he gave a dismissive snort before quickly stripping off and tossing his clothes carelessly around the room.

Good lord, he was a truly magnificent sight and all hers, if only for a few short hours. For once Cassie refused to question anything and just enjoy the here and now. She met his piercing stare and sucked in a sharp breath as his hand moved straight to the center of her desire, stroking and probing.

'Got a problem with my direct method?' Jay murmured as he eased two fingers inside her welcoming warmth.

Cassie's reply was a gasp of pleasure as he pressed deeper and leaned over to take the tip of one aching breast into his mouth; combined with a sudden twist of his fingers it pushed her over the edge and she convulsed helplessly around him. His arousal pressed insistently against her inner thigh and she shifted to rub against his silken length.

'You want more, darlin' girl?' Jay's soft laugh let something loose inside Cassie and she reached out to caress him. His neck muscles corded with tension as she squeezed and stroked until finally he roughly pushed her hands away. She loved breaking his control.

Jay leaned across and grabbed a packet from the bedside drawer, and her blood rushed hot and needy at the sight of him as he centered himself, held her hips still and thrust hard. She took him in with a loud exhalation and rose to meet him, instantly moving in sync with his rhythm. Jay grabbed a handful of her hair, jerking her head up to meet his electric gaze.

'Look in the mirror, Cassie, watch us come together.'

His fierce words excited her and she gazed upwards, feeling the first stirrings begin as he shifted position, moving deeper and faster until, with one final thrust, he tipped her into a place of swirling ecstasy and she couldn't take her eyes from the symphony of their bodies entwinded together. Suddenly, Jay stiffened and collapsed into his own release, his skin burning hot and sated against hers.

'Tired enough to sleep now?' he drawled with a wicked smile, still throbbing inside her.

'You're a wicked man.' Cassie stared into his sparkling eyes and let her hands rove over his gorgeous body, savoring the sheer strength and masculine power under her fingers.

'I'd stay inside you all night if I thought you wouldn't get crushed.' Jay whispered and Cassie couldn't answer, afraid to say too much as he rolled back onto the bed. 'I'd love you to stay but I guess you'd better go back to your own room.'

'You're right, unfortunately.' Cassie sighed, surprised again by his thoughtfulness.

She reluctantly moved out of the comfort of his arms and headed for the door, turning to blow him a kiss before she sneaked back to her lonely room, where she fell asleep with Jay's scent clinging to her skin, clutching a pillow as a poor substitute for his strong, warm body.

# 8

Cassie surfaced from a deep sleep at the sound of Jay's agitated voice outside her bedroom door, talking into his mobile. The conversation stopped and her door was flung open.

'The police will be here in about half an hour. Get dressed and wake Sam. I have to make a phone call.'

Being ordered around irritated her but she bit back a sharp retort; he hadn't backed away this time. Maybe they'd prove Tony wrong after all.

Jay ran back to his room and returning carrying one of his blue dress shirts.

'Tell Sam to wear this. It'll be a touch too big but it'll cover his tattoo. Get that last earring out too and make sure he showers and flattens his hair.'

'What the devil do you think — ?'

He grabbed her arm. 'Do you want

the police to take one look at him and know they've got a teenage drug pusher or do you want them to wonder if maybe they've made a mistake?'

Cassie snatched the shirt and stalked off. She didn't have to like the fact that he was right.

* * *

'Samuel James Moore. We'd like you to come to the station for questioning related to Miss Lindy Retallick.'

Cassie's arm tightened around Sam's shoulder.

'But I didn't — '

'Sam. Remember?' Jay's low, deep words shut Sam up. 'Detective Inspector Corbin, I'm Jay Burton, a friend of the family. Sam will be happy to come to the station at a time convenient to him and his lawyer.'

Cassie's heart raced. Nobody she knew dared to speak to the police that way.

'Lawyer? Got someone lined up have

you?' The detective mocked and a dangerous smirk crossed Jay's face.

'Yes, we do. Sam is a client of Mr Julian Warrington. QC.'

'You're shi — ' His face flamed. 'Sorry, Ms Moore.'

'Are you acquainted with Mr Warrington, Inspector?' Jay asked quietly but his innocent words didn't fool Cassie; at his most polite, Jay was deadly.

'We've had dealings. If three o'clock this afternoon will suit, call me at this number, and if it doesn't we'll reschedule.' The detective thrust a business card at Jay, poked his colleague in the arm and they left.

'So Mr Cool-and-Lethal, what was all that about?' Cassie questioned and Jay grinned like a mischievous child.

'Mr Julian Warrington is the top criminal defense lawyer in the country and wins almost all his big, high profile cases. That copper knows he's in deep trouble because Julian wouldn't normally touch the case of an ordinary teenage drug dealer.'

'I'm not a drug dealer,' Sam glared.

'We know that, Sam, but they don't,' Jay explained patiently.

Cassie still didn't get it. 'So why is he helping Sam?'

Jay pulled her into his arms. 'Because he was another roommate in my sordid Clapham days, along with Tony, and we've stayed friends. He owes me, several times over. He probably wouldn't have his law license if I hadn't kept him out of trouble when he was a rowdy young man.'

'You're a proper Irish devil, you know that don't you?' Cassie laughed out loud.

'Turns you on, doesn't it?' Jay whispered in her ear and his hands tightened around her waist.

Cassie flung her hair back and pushed out of his arms. 'I'll see if there's anything to eat in the kitchen.'

'It'll be a waste of time. There's a Tesco Metro near where we had dinner. Take my credit card and get some things. I'll call Julian over here to meet Sam.'

* * *

Cassie stepped back into Jay's flat and her bags were taken away by a short, wiry man with black-rimmed glasses and friendly eyes.

'Good morning. You must be the famous Cassie. I've never met a woman who could tie Jay up in knots before. Most impressive. Julian Warrington, at your service.'

'Don't listen to him. He's a lawyer.' Jay interjected. 'They wouldn't know the truth if they fall over it.' Jay cuffed Julian around the head, the bags dropped to the floor and they scrapped like five-year-olds on the school playground. In less than two minutes Jay had him pinned and begging for mercy. He sprung to his feet and hauled his old friend up, dusting off Julian's obviously expensive black pinstripe suit.

'Have you children quite finished?'

Cassie folded her arms and glared. 'I'll get lunch ready if you can behave. Will sandwiches be all right?'

'That'll be fine, darlin'. Give us the strength to beat down the police later, right Julian?' Jay's eyes danced with the challenge.

'Absolutely. I'll coach Sam on what to say and we'll wipe the floor with them. This makes a pleasant change from mass murderers and terrorists.' Julian grinned.

'I'm happy my son's misfortune is affording you both so much enjoyment.'

Julian straightened his bent glasses and fixed her with his dark green eyes. 'My dear Ms Moore, my client's problems are never a source of humor and I'm very sorry if our behaviour upset you.' He nodded towards Jay. 'The problem is this man is a hopeless case. I hope one day to reform him into a productive citizen, but . . . ' The slight twist to his mouth struggled to burst into a full smile, but he held it in check.

Cassie cracked. 'I didn't mean to

come across as — '

'Pompous. Pretentious. Supercilious . . . ?'

'Don't push your luck, Jay Burton.'

They all gave up and laughed together.

'You're all bloody mad.' Sam muttered, glaring at them all.

'Sorry, mate.' Jay rested a hand on Sam's arm. 'We shouldn't have messed around. You stay here and talk to Julian while I help your mother fix lunch.'

In the kitchen Jay slid his hands around Cassie's waist, burying his face in her soft, perfumed curls. 'I am such a jerk. I haven't a clue why you bother with me.'

She wriggled around and laid her cheek against his chest. 'Fishing for compliments again, are you?'

'Far from it. I don't deserve any. I didn't mean — '

Her finger on his lips silenced him. 'I know. Sam will survive a little humour. He hasn't laughed much the last few years. Now take your hands off me and get drinks for everyone while I finish making the sandwiches.'

Jay slid one hand under her skirt, teasing up the outside of her bare thigh and tracing feathery strokes on her smooth skin. 'Are you sure about that?'

With a giggle she pushed him away. 'Do what you're told. You'll have to wait until later.'

He gave her a last, lingering kiss making her moan softly.

'I'm not the only one who'll have to wait,' he said as he strolled to the fridge.

* * *

'No problem, we'll see you there.' Jay hung up and turned back to Cassie.

'Well?' Her dark, tormented eyes tied a knot inside him. She'd practically wrung her hands while they waited to hear from Julian. It'd taken all Jay's Irish charm to convince her to stay with him and let Sam to go with his lawyer to the police station.

'It went fine. Sam hasn't been

charged. The police will talk to Lindy when her doctor says it's OK and as long as Julian convinces them there's enough doubt they won't prosecute. Julian's taking Sam to the hospital so we'll meet them there.'

'Thank you.' A tear slid quietly down her cheek and Jay lifted her chin to meet his gaze.

'We're in this together, remember?' He stumbled over the words and for several long seconds she didn't answer.

'Yes.' Cassie breathed and Jay's heart flipped.

'I'll get my keys.'

That was the best he could come up with? He was grateful she didn't push him any further. It was one of the things he loved most about her.

Loved? Jay pushed the idea away.

# 9

'Question my daughter? You must be mad. She nearly died because of that boy. You've no right to talk to her.' Doctor Retallick blustered.

Jay tightened his hold on Cassie's hand as they turned the corner and walked into Peter Retallick and the same policemen they'd dealt with earlier.

'This is all your bloody fault.' Lindy's father jabbed a finger hard into Jay's chest. 'You and your fancy lawyer. I suppose you think he'll get the boy off. You don't intimidate me.'

Jay tensed, itching to punch the man.

'Don't,' Cassie murmured.

'Doctor Retallick, we understand your concern but we must talk to Lindy,' the policeman explained. 'The doctor says she's well enough for a short chat. If you want a lawyer present you're entitled to one.'

'Fine. Go ahead but if she has a setback afterwards it'll be your fault.' Retallick stormed off down the corridor.

'Come on, let's find Sam and wait, we can't do much else.' Jay urged and Cassie clung to him. He rather liked how it felt.

Sam raised his head when they walked into the waiting room, his dark eyes glistening with relief — not something Jay often saw in another person's eyes at the sight of him.

'Hi, Sam. Where's Mr Warrington?'

'He had to leave but he said to call when we hear anything.' He hesitated. 'He's alright for a lawyer.'

His shy half-smile allowed Jay to give one of his own in return.

'Yeah. He's not bad.'

'He told me a few stories about you.' Jay hadn't seen a teasing glint in Sam's eyes before. 'Well, I could tell a few in return, so he'd better be careful.'

'I might share them with Mum later.'

Sam threatened with a broad grin.

'You don't want a fast ride in the BMW then?' Jay pulled his chain in return and Sam threw up his hands in surrender.

'Good to see him behaving for once.' Jay hugged Cassie.

Suddenly Amanda Retallick, her eyes reddened from crying, stepped into the room and Jay quickly checked for her husband.

'You're safe, Mr Burton, Peter's still with Lindy and the police. She's signing a statement.' Her pale skin was filmed with a sheen of sweat.

Jay touched her arm. 'Sit down, please. Can I get you a drink of water? You don't look well.'

She almost collapsed in the chair and her pale blue eyes glassed over with tears. 'I came to apologise since no-one else in my family will.'

Turning to face Sam she haltingly carried on. 'Lindy told us the truth. Finally. She admitted buying the drugs herself and said you wouldn't take any.

I doubt they'll catch the person who sold it to her but I'm very sorry you got dragged into this.'

'She didn't make me come to London. I wanted to as much as her.' Sam asserted.

'Thank you. She's a spoilt girl and that's our fault. We're taking her home tomorrow and then . . . ' Amanda sighed.

'Parenting is hard isn't it? This has been a wake-up call for me, too,' Cassie said thoughtfully.

'Sam, do you want to see Lindy before we leave?' Jay wanted the boy to think carefully before he answered.

'Yeah, I do to make sure she's OK.'

Jay admired his bravery. 'We'll be outside in the car when you're finished.'

'We could come with —

Jay stopped Cassie with a sharp nod of his head. One of the ways a boy learnt to become a man was by doing tough things alone. Women couldn't protect you from everything, Jay thought — especially yourself.

In the car Cassie snuggled into Jay. 'I don't care what you say, Jay Burton, you're a good man.'

Her light, floral perfume distracted him so much he almost put the car in first gear instead of reverse. Jay took her face in his hands and stopped any more praises with a long, deep kiss, savoring her sweet taste.

'Can't you two keep your hands off each other? Wait till I'm in bed or I'll puke,' Sam grunted in fake disgust.

'All over my fine leather upholstery? I don't think so. Cassie, your charming son believes he's getting a lift with us. What do you think?' He asked with a grin.

'He needs to be a lot more appreciative. If he behaves like a little boy we'll put him to bed at six like a toddler.'

Sam tried to smile but plainly wasn't sure about the whole bantering around thing, so Jay gave in. 'Come on. Hop in.

I think tonight calls for pizza.'

He empathised with Sam's confusion and mentally crossed his fingers that he wouldn't screw up again.

\* \* \*

A shirtless Jay, wearing only black boxers, was rather more than Cassie was used to first thing in the morning. He leaned against the counter drinking a mug of tea and nibbling a piece of buttered toast. It took all her feeble self-control not to throw herself at him.

'I'm sorry I have to go into work. I can drive you and Sam back to Cornwall tomorrow if you like? I'll try to be back by seven tonight but don't wait for me to eat. I'm often late and probably won't think to call. I'm not used to . . . ' his voice trailed away.

Maybe he wasn't as calm as he seemed and the thought cheered Cassie. 'Tomorrow will be fine. I'd offer to get the train but I can't deprive Sam of riding in your car. I'll let Mum and

Dad know. Tony's been checking on them for me.'

Jay put down his mug. 'I'd better get dressed.' He didn't move, his eyes roaming over her. Even from where she stood, Cassie felt the heat from his bare chest and reached out to touch the wisps of crisp, dark hair.

Next thing his mouth was on hers and his hands slid up under her t-shirt, stroking her heated skin as he dragged her down the hall, pushed her inside his bedroom and locked the door. Jay yanked her nightdress off over her head and pressed her back against the wall, then freed himself from his boxers and pushed himself between her trembling legs.

'What about Sam?' she gasped.

'He's fast asleep. I'll be quick and you'll be quiet.'

Cassie wanted to argue but with one swift move he had already slid inside her, filling her like no-one else ever had. His fingers dug into the flesh of her backside as he held her in place and pounded into her. She could barely keep up and as he pushed her over the edge she bit back a scream.

'Hell, Cassie . . . '

Jay throbbed from his own release and collapsed against her, the weight of his heavy body the only thing keeping her from dissolving into a puddle on the carpet.

Suddenly shock filled his eyes and he jerked out of her. 'I forgot to use anything . . . '

Cassie laid a finger on his lips. 'It's alright. I'm on the pill, although I haven't been with anybody for a long time.'

His smile returned and he stroked her cheek. 'You drive all reason from me, darlin' girl. I really must get dressed now. You certainly know how to make a man want to leave work early.'

Cassie pulled her nightdress back on and waited for her heart to slow back down to normal then fled back to the kitchen before she gave in to the desire to lure him to stay longer.

Fifteen minutes later Jay emerged ready for the day. This was 'London Jay' in a perfectly cut dark gray suit with a faint pinstripe, immaculate pale blue shirt, dark blue silk tie, and highly polished black shoes. His dark hair, sleekly tamed, shone under the lights. She stepped towards him, bringing her close enough to catch the scent of freshly showered man overlaid with his delicious musky cologne.

'What magazine did you step out of?'

He beamed, instantly returning to the real Jay, picked up his laptop case and slipped his mobile in his trouser pocket.

'You've got my work phone number. Ring if there's any problem. If I don't answer leave a message and I'll get back to you. You can sort of see my office from here.'

Jay pulled her out on the balcony and pointed to the right. 'That's One Canada Square, otherwise known as the Canary Wharf Tower. It's the tallest building in the UK and where good old

Solomon and Gates imprison their employees until they make sufficient money to gain their release.'

His smile dissipated and she took his oversized hand in hers, loving the difference between them. 'I'll be your Rapunzel. I'll let down my hair and you can climb to freedom.'

Jay's eyes bored into her. 'You have no idea, do you?' He pressed a wistfully sad kiss onto her mouth and disappeared.

After she'd washed and dressed, Cassie gathered her courage and returned to the kitchen.

'Sam?'

He raised his eyes from the plate of toast he was busy demolishing. 'Yeah, what?'

She almost wished she'd waited until Jay was back to be a buffer between them.

'We need to talk.'

'Lecture time is it? I thought you'd gone too many days without one. Shall I save your energy and do it for you?

Things are going to be different when we go home. I'm going back to school or getting a job. No more underage drinking. You want to know where I'm going and what time I'm getting back. How am I doing so far?'

Sam's black anger scared her but she'd gone too far to stop now. 'Is that unreasonable?'

For once he didn't reply straight away and a glimmer of hope snaked through Cassie when he couldn't meet her steady gaze. 'Is it, Sam?' She placed her right hand firmly on top of his.

'S'pose not.'

'Did you say . . . ?' Cassie leaned in closer to him.

Sam flung back out of the chair tossing her hand away roughly. 'Yes. You happy now are you?'

He stormed from the kitchen into the bedroom, slamming the door hard behind him.

Nevertheless, for the first time in way too long, Cassie breathed properly.

# 10

Jay kissed the soft nape of her neck and Cassie sighed. 'You think I did the right thing?'

'Yes, I do but I don't envy you following through.'

'You don't think I will?' Cassie jerked away.

'Oh darlin', I didn't say that.' He slid across the crumpled sheets and tried to get hold of her again but she sat up.

'You didn't need to. I'm tired of everyone thinking I'm a lousy mother and telling me so in no uncertain terms — especially people who are childless themselves,' Cassie snapped.

Jay held up his hands in a gesture of submission.

'Leave it for now,' she sighed. 'I need to concentrate on Sam for a while. I don't have the time or the energy for . . . for whatever this is.' She gestured at the two of them.

'Are you dumping me?'

'I . . . I don't want to be without you in my life, but I don't see where you fit in . . . do you?' Cassie asked sadly and indecision tightened his smile.

She struggled to steady her voice. 'I'm not going to ask for something you're not ready for, Jay.' She sighed. 'I shouldn't say this but I'm going to anyway . . . I love you, Jay. I think I've loved you since the moment we first met.'

Jay couldn't quite meet her eyes.

'Don't worry. I don't expect you to say it back. Our lives are so opposite I can't see it ever working anyway.'

'Cassie.' Jay sucked in a deep, heavy breath. 'I don't know if I'm even capable of loving anyone, but I care for you more than any woman I've ever known. I love being with you — and I don't mean only in bed — we're good together . . . But you deserve better than me and I'm not ready for the next step. I'm not being fair because I don't want to lose you either.'

'Decent men aren't exactly queuing up to date me, you know. Single mothers of troublesome teenage sons with dependent elderly parents don't have to fight off men with a stick.'

Jay pulled her back into his arms. 'Then they must be mad. I don't care if you've a whole slew of family problems. It may be clichéd but the problem is me, not you.'

'I'm not asking for a commitment today, next week, or even next year. I only want to know if you're open to the possibility and we can take it a day at a time. No promises either side.'

It was a huge chance but one of them had to take it and he was too scared. His unshaven jaw rubbed against her cheek as he slid in to kiss her.

'You're amazing. That'll work for me . . . if you're sure?'

'All I ask is faithfulness. If you decide you can't or don't want to be with me exclusively anymore, you must tell me. I might cry, in fact I probably will, but you'll have to deal with that.'

Jay's eyes were silver in the bright sunlight streaming in through the unshielded windows. 'I can promise that.'

She smiled, surprisingly shyly, and it twisted at his heart.

'Well, it's time to get dressed and burn up the road to Cornwall and sort out more of the family problems you said didn't bother you. Time to put your money where your mouth is.'

His warm lips pressed against her throat, rapidly heading south. 'I'd rather put my mouth somewhere else.'

And he did.

* * *

'Hey, Eamon. Can you pick me up at the airport about two this afternoon?' Jay packed a small bag and listened to his brother's questions at the same time. 'No. Everything's fine. Any problem with me coming to stay for a few days?'

He'd barely caught his breath after

driving, way too fast, back from Cornwall. It was the whole damn promise thing. He understood why Cassie had asked but hated being pinned down. He didn't intend on being unfaithful, wasn't even attracted to any other women but still . . .

Jay turned off his mobile and sat on the bed. He couldn't shake from his mind what he'd overheard Sam saying to Cassie.

'What'd you expect? He's not going to hang around this dump longer than he has to, is he? I suppose he told you he loved you and you believed it — stupid woman,' he'd said.

Cassie had tried to defend him, saying he'd never told her any such thing, but Sam had carried on with, 'Maybe he didn't say that exactly but something made you think he was staying so don't lie. We'll do fine without him.'

The last thing he'd heard was Sam thumping up the stairs and Cassie's gulping, sad tears. Jay had closed the door very gently as he had left and never looked back.

Now Jay had to make one more phone call before his flight.

'John. I'll sort things out properly on Monday, but you should know now that I'm resigning.' Jay held the receiver away so he couldn't hear his boss's angry words as clearly. 'Yes, I am grateful for everything but I'm making changes in my life, John. Big changes.' He hung up while John Gates was still speaking, not a smart career move.

Jay stripped off the black trousers and green polo shirt he'd traveled in, pulled out a pair of old jeans and a t-shirt, plus a worn blue sweater for the inevitable cool evening, and was ready.

He wouldn't get in touch with Cassie again until he was sure. She deserved that much.

* * *

Eamon scrutinised Jay across the messy supper table with their mother's shrewd sky-blue eyes, innocent on the surface but deadly accurate in whatever they observed.

'I didn't just come because I wanted a weekend away, you know.' Jay announced.

'Really?' Eamon put more into that one word than most people could put into a whole speech.

Jay cleared his throat, almost nervously. 'I've resigned from Solomon and Gates. I have to go back and sort things out, admin stuff, but I'm done with them — and no, I don't know what I'm going to do next.'

Eamon stroked a hand through his thinning light brown hair. 'What brought this on?'

There was the truth. There were lies. And there were a million things in between.

'I've been . . . sort of restless for a while. The challenge has gone. Mum . . . Mum dying sort of . . . ' His voice trailed away and he choked back tears.

'Made you think? Hallelujah, Pat, lad

— and about time too! You haven't been happy in years. It's a shame she had to die for you to realise it but some of us are born stubborn. Stay as long as you want. I can always use an extra pair of hands around the farm. Of course you'll have to drag your sorry ass out of bed at five for the milking.'

Jay shrugged. 'I'm always up early to do an hour in the gym before work.'

Eamon reached over and squeezed Jay's bicep. 'Yeah, well, suppose you're not too soft for a London boy.'

In return Jay punched Eamon lightly in the chest.

Mary snatched hold of both their hands and glared. 'Stop it right now, you two. Eamon Burton, you're a middle-aged father of three sons and supposed to set them a good example of how a man behaves. We don't need the bad influence of this delinquent brother of yours.'

Mary threw a cheeky smile in Jay's direction.

He had never seen the attraction of a

solid, sensible woman like Mary before. She'd never been further than Dublin in her life and was deeply rooted in her family and the friends she'd had since schooldays. In a flash he realised this sort of woman grounded a man and made him better, complete.

Eamon smiled at his wife, apologising with his eyes and a soft kiss on her cheek and Jay glanced away.

'It's been a long day. I'm heading off to bed so I can drag my sorry ass out in the morning.' He stood and pushed the chair away, unable to be with them any longer.

'Your ass doesn't look sorry to me.' Mary's green eyes roved over him and sparkled with mischief.

'Hey, that's my baby brother you're talking about, you married woman!' Eamon struggled to sound stern.

'When you drool over one of those supermodels you tell me it's all right to look so long as you don't touch and that's exactly what I'm doing.'

Jay held up his hands in surrender.

'Maybe I shouldn't stay after all. I don't want to be responsible for breaking up your marriage.' He laughed hard and deep and it felt good.

'Aw, go on with you. See you tomorrow. Go and get some sleep.' Eamon ordered.

* * *

Three days of hard labor settled one thing in Jay's mind — he didn't plan to become a farmer any time soon, but nevertheless Eamon's life tugged at him.

The boys were what Jay most envied. Will, Seamus, and Andy were like replicas of he, Eamon and Colum as kids. The little devils were on the go from early morning until they collapsed exhausted at night with all their surplus energy channeled into school, farm chores, football and church. Jay realised that their life was what Sam needed because Sam was what happened to a directionless boy. An idea mulled in his head giving him plenty to think on while he walked alone for miles.

And at the back of everything was Cassie. He couldn't allow himself to make a decision until everything else was straight. The next time he approached her what he said and what she heard must be in absolute sync.

His whole family were coming over for Sunday supper before he left in the morning. He'd wear his suit one last time before he changed his life completely forever.

★ ★ ★

'I'm calling Jay later, any message?'

Cassie met Tony's guileless expression and strived to hold her voice steady. They hadn't mentioned Jay in weeks.

'I don't think so. I've nothing to say to him.'

'Sorry, I didn't mean to upset you,' he apologised.

'I'm not upset but there's nothing left

for us to talk about. I'm going out back to sort the new books.'

The shop door bell rang and a man approached the counter. The yogurt she'd eaten for lunch rose in Cassie's throat.

'Long time no see.' Pete Wilson's gravelly voice was the same but the lean young man with the long, satiny black hair was gone as if he'd never been; his coal black eyes were darker than ever, set against his pale skin and although still only in his mid-30s his now brutally short hair was snowy white.

'Changed a bit, have I?' Bitterness seeped from every pore and she shivered.

Tony touched her elbow. 'Would you like an early lunch?'

He must wonder who Pete was but Cassie couldn't speak, let alone explain. 'Alright.'

She turned to the man who had changed her life. 'If it's OK with you we can go to the pub down the road.'

Pete nodded briefly. Maybe he didn't

know what to say either.

When they were seated in the pub Cassie found she had no appetite at all and her vegetable soup cooled in the bowl while she covertly watched him eat with his hand held protectively around the plate and his eyes fixed on the food. Five minutes of silent eating and he was done.

'Sorry. I'm not used to being able to take my time yet.'

His quick slice of a smile sharpened her memories of the irresistible charm that had got her in so much trouble all those years ago.

'Cassie,' he hesitated for a moment before carrying on. 'You've done a great job with Sam.'

'Sam? How would you know? You left when he was this big.' Her hands spread a foot apart.

Pete's expression turned wary. 'Didn't he tell you?'

'Tell me what?'

'I spoke to him yesterday outside school. Gave him a lift home.' A challenge lurked behind his blank, dark eyes.

'Have you been stalking him?'

Pete gave a rough laugh. 'Stalking? I wanted to see my son and there's no court order against it.'

His attitude riled Cassie. Who the hell did he think he was?

'Would you like me to get one?' she snapped. 'It shouldn't be difficult. After all you ran off when I was pregnant. You've spent half of his life locked up for drug dealing and assault. I don't think any judge will see you as an asset to Sam's life.'

The sharp words spewed out before she could think straight.

Pete sipped his orange juice. 'Don't be too sure. I'm rehabilitated. I've got a degree in social work and don't touch alcohol or drugs now. I started a job last month with the local council, helping troubled youth.'

She forced down a spoonful of soup and said nothing.

'The way I see it they might even

consider me a good influence on a boy who's been allowed to run wild. I understand Sam's been in trouble with the law and was recently retrieved from an escapade in London involving a teenage girl and some bad Ecstasy.' He gave a sly smile. 'I don't see me being forbidden to see Sam at all. In fact, if I'm patient and wait a few more months I bet I can get joint custody.' Pete patted his flat stomach. 'I'm still hungry. Fancy some treacle tart? That always used to be your favorite.'

'How dare you!' Cassie hissed. 'I did the best I could. Don't think you're going to march in here and play happy families after what you've done.'

Pete threw up his hands in surrender. 'I'm sorry, Cassie. I didn't mean to imply you didn't try with Sam. I'm not here to make trouble I just want to get to know my son. I want to make amends for the way I treated you both. If you'll let me.'

No way could she allow one sliver of trust to sneak into her heart. Not again.

She must be careful. 'I'll talk to Sam later. Does he know how to get in touch with you?'

'No. I told him I'd have to speak to you first. Here's my card. All I ask is that you let him decide for himself.'

'If you can be a . . . a friend to Sam he could do with that. Don't expect too much though,' she cautioned.

Pete's jaw tightened. 'Expect too much? I expect nothing. I learnt that the hard way.'

His hands, scarred from the fights he'd never avoided, gripped the edge of the table. This man wasn't the teenage boy who'd casually seduced her and left with no qualms, but she wasn't stupid enough to have anything to do with him a second time around.

'Yes, well, and whose fault is it? You'll get no sympathy from me. I'll pass on your message to Sam and that's it.'

Pete nodded. 'I have to get back to work now.' He stood and held out his hand. 'Thanks, Cassie. I appreciate you listening.'

She steeled herself but the touch of his firm hand, hands that had destroyed her sanity in the past, was only a normal handshake with a stranger. Cassie breathed again.

\* \* \*

Jay knotted his tie, flattened down a rogue hair. Sixteen years ago the suit had been a cheap off-the-peg, the tie one of Eamon's cast-offs, and the black shoes well-polished to cover the scratches. A little different from today's elegant attire, but the stomach clenching nerves were the same.

He was either making the best decision of his life or royally screwing up. Would Cassie think he was mad or would she understand why he'd given up his lifestyle? Jay didn't know if he'd even get to ask after the way they'd parted company.

But he mustn't think of her today because this wasn't being done for her. It was for him and him alone.

A couple of hours later, the real estate agent left with a smile on her face. The economy might be dodgy but apparently there were plenty of young traders with deep pockets who'd love this place as the seal on their success. Exactly the way it had been for him once.

Did he turn up at the Blue Room tonight for the farewell do hastily thrown together by his co-workers? They'd pester him for explanations that Jay didn't intend giving and he'd end up drunk and second-guessing himself.

He wouldn't tell Brian until it was a fait accompli and two hours later his car was replaced by a five-year-old Volvo.

'Hey, Tony, I need advice.'

His old friend would get it, after all he'd turned his own life around. 'I've quit my job, sold the car, and put the flat up for sale. What do I do now?' His attempt to laugh fell flat.

'Don't do things by half, do you?' Tony gasped.

'I want to do something useful. Money's not an issue.'

'Only you could say that, you black-hearted devil.' Tony's teasing remark broke the ice and they both laughed.

'You thinking about getting away for a while then?'

'Yeah, but not back with you. No offence but I can't . . . '

'Not here, you moron. I meant out of the country.'

'Determined to keep me away from Cassie, are you?' A shard of something close to jealousy shot through Jay.

'You seriously need to sort yourself out so the answer to your dumb question would be a yes,' Tony said patiently. 'Have you heard of Voluntary Service Overseas?'

'Isn't that some sort of do-gooders thing helping poor people?' Jay responded.

'Oh, great attitude, I'm glad I suggested this. Shut up a minute and listen. I've got friends who've taken part and had an incredible experience. Ray went to Ghana for two years — '

'Two years? That's a bit drastic, isn't it?'

'Don't worry. I wouldn't inflict you on anyone for that long. They've got a scheme of specialist assignments, usually only a few months, for people who are experts in a skill they need. I'm pretty sure your financial genius could be used. You have to pass some interviews but I'm sure you could con them into thinking you're a decent person.'

'That might be alright.'

'Go online, the website's got all the details.' Tony cleared his throat.' By the way Cassie is fine.'

'I didn't ask.'

'The big news is Sam's father turned up. Sober and respectable and wants to play a part in the boy's life. He was eyeing up your Cassie too.'

Jay's gut ached from the punch of Tony's words. 'That could be good for the boy. But she's not 'my Cassie.' I gave up that right when I left . . . if I ever had it.'

'Yes, you did.' Tony waited. 'In case it interests you she didn't respond to his overtures.'

'I'm no good for her, Tony. I couldn't do it when it came down to the wire. Maybe one day it'll be different but . . . '

'Hmm. Well, let me know what happens with the VSO thing.'

'I will and thanks. You're a better friend than I am.'

'I'll agree with you there. Now go save the world.'

Jay needed to save himself first — but at least he realised that at last.

# 11

Cassie idly removed books from the box on the floor and scattered them over the table instead of efficiently sorting them into piles.

'Daydreaming? Must be a good one.' Tony held out a mug of tea to her and she blushed. 'It wouldn't feature sparkling Irish eyes, would it?'

She flamed a deeper shade of scarlet and bit her lip.

'Has he been in touch?' Tony's green eyes studied her.

'I'm sure you know he hasn't. He's your friend after all.'

'Jay's in Birmingham this weekend.' Tony said casually, taking a sip of tea.

'And that interests me, why?' Cassie asked with a calmness she didn't feel.

Tony gave her a strange unreadable look. 'It's his briefing session before he leaves for Zambia in a couple of weeks.'

211

'OK, you obviously want to tell me something so I'll keep you happy and ask. Why is he going to Zambia?'

'He quit his job a couple of months ago. He's going on a short-term assignment with the Voluntary Service Overseas. He'll be gone about three months.'

'I hope you're not implying he's done this because of me?'

Tony's gentle smile made her guilty for her sharp tongue. 'No, let's just say that you made him think, something Jay's avoided for a while. Losing his mother shook him up badly.'

He gave her shoulder a comforting squeeze. 'I just thought you'd like to know.'

Cassie brushed away an escaped tear. 'He let me down, Tony. But ten times worse were all the promises he made to Sam and Sam's been disappointed enough. Now Pete's hanging around all the time and I'm afraid he'll do the same as Jay did.'

Tony drew in a deep breath before

carrying on. 'I wouldn't let you or Sam down ever . . . think about that.'

He took Cassie's hands firmly in his and refused to let her avoid his searching gaze. The clear desire in his eyes stunned her to silence and Tony's right hand trembled as he reached towards her face and one finger stroked a hot path down her cheek. He bent and pressed his warm, firm lips against her mouth as his arm slid around her waist, pulling her closer. His tongue teased her lips but she didn't — couldn't — respond.

Abruptly Tony let go and stepped away. 'I never learn, do I?' he said, a hint of bitterness lacing his sad tone.

But it didn't matter if he was right, she couldn't pretend an attraction that simply wasn't there. 'Maybe it would be better for us both if I stopped working here,' Cassie murmured quietly.

Tony's face filled with horror. 'Oh God, no. I'm sorry. Please don't. I can't lose my best friend.' He struggled to smile.

'I need a friend more than anything.' That was the truth.

'Good. How about going out at the weekend like we used to?' he suggested. 'No kissing, I promise.'

'I'd like that. I expect Pete will be happy to stay there with Sam and keep an eye on Mum and Dad. I'll check and get back to you. Now go and do something useful while I check these books.' She shooed him away and breathed again.

* * *

Cassie watched from the front door as Sam and Pete walked toward the house, heads bent close and talking non-stop. In a second the first words out of her son's mouth would be, 'Can Dad stay for dinner?'

And just what had he done to deserve it? If only she could let go of her resentment.

'Hey, Mum . . . ?'

'Yes, there's enough beef pie and yes,

214

Pete can stay for tea.'

Sam ran on into the house but Pete lingered next to her on the step, his fingers resting lightly on her arm. It was all she could do not to pull away.

'I appreciate it, Cassie, and I don't just mean dinner. I didn't mean to drop back in your life but after I saw Sam the first time . . . I can't make up for what I did but if I can help Sam in any way now I will. If it turns out that the best thing is for me not to see him I'd hate it but I'd stay away if that's what he wants.'

'I'll not send you away unless you hurt Sam.' Cassie's voice softened. 'I'm struggling not to project my bad memories onto him but I can't let myself remember any of the good ones with you either, for my own sake.'

Pete's dark eyes roved over her face. 'I'm surprised you're not married or with someone.'

'I have too much baggage to be much of a catch. You made me wary of men.' Cassie grimaced then pulled herself together. 'Come on, dinner's nearly ready.'

* * *

'You want to watch him.' Cassie's mother nodded towards Pete, playing cards with Sam at the kitchen table. Her mother's cynical glance spoke volumes. 'You can't see it can you? He's using the boy to get back in with you. He's not to be trusted any more now than he was sixteen years ago.'

Cassie turned away and studied Pete. He talked intently to Sam, occasionally pushing one hand through his hair, the shocking white of it still catching her unawares. He stilled and swiveled around to face her, his penetrating stare bringing a rush of blood to her face.

'Care to join us?' he asked with a challenge in his voice.

Her mother was wrong because Cassie recognised exactly what Pete was up to. Some days she wondered if it'd

216

be so terrible? Pete's occasional tentative touches on her arm or shoulder made it crystal clear what he had in mind.

Instantly Jay's face flooded into her memory, those incredible silvery blue eyes, his wicked smile and the kindness that lay beneath it all. The second she said yes to Pete, Jay had to be history and she couldn't do it. Not yet.

'No, thanks. Sam's got homework to do.'

A flare of anger lit up Pete's eyes but he quickly covered it with a smile. 'I'd best be going then. See you Saturday, Sam?'

'Yeah, my game's at ten.'

'I'll be there and don't worry about the evening, Cassie. I'll stay here so you can go out.'

Cassie grimaced. He made her sound so selfish. She'd devoted her life to Sam for sixteen years and now Pete waltzed back in and took on the role of Wonder Dad.

She held on to her temper. 'Thanks. I

appreciate it.' She squeezed the words out along with the vestige of a smile.

By the time Pete left and Cassie sat down to drink her coffee, it was stone cold. She put it down again as Sam sat beside her.

'Have you heard from him or is that a stupid question?'

'Who?'

'Who'd you think? Irish lover boy. Mr Love-em-and-dump-em.'

'You're not being fair, Sam, Jay was good to us.'

He snorted. 'I'm not being fair? Dad said . . . '

'How does your father know about Jay?'

Sam's face flushed. 'I might've mentioned him.'

'You shouldn't have. It's none of his business.'

'It could be.' Sam answered right back.

'Sam.' She rested her hand on his, she'd let this drift on and it was time to be honest with herself as well as everyone else. 'It's not going to be.'

Sam pulled away and jumped up from the sofa.

'Why not? I think you still love him and I know he loves you. What's so awful about the idea?'

She chose her words with care. 'It's good to see you two together. I loved Pete once in a young, teenage way and I can't regret it because of you.' Something lightened inside Cassie and it was nothing to do with Jay. 'But we're different people now and I think he's just clinging to the past because of you.'

Sam slumped down onto the sofa and Cassie dared to put her arm around his rigid shoulders and hold on until he relaxed. His face pressed into her and sad, hot tears soaked through her blouse. With her free right hand she stroked his soft hair, murmuring the old motherly platitude that it would be alright.

Hopefully he didn't notice she had her fingers crossed.

* ★ ★

Jay shoved the small airline pillow under his neck and tried to rest, but too much crowded his mind. Another three hours and the long flight to Johannesburg would be over, he'd have a short layover and another two hour flight before he landed in Lusaka. In theory he'd be met by Pierre La Pont, who'd drive him to Choma, then his new job would start.

As soon as he heard the mandate — to be a troubleshooter, hit the ground running, and achieve a lot in a short space of time — Jay knew he'd found the right place. The VSO people questioned him deeply because he guessed they didn't get too many successful bankers, outside of company backed placements, willing to chuck everything in for several months. Luckily this job came up and he fitted the bill perfectly so they hadn't been able to turn him down.

He got out his information packet

and re-read it, although he knew every word by heart. Jay's tired eyes began to close and he let them because then he'd hopefully feel his mother's presence again. Every lecture he sat through, every meeting he attended, waiting at the doctor's office for his shots, and out buying sensible, nerdy shorts, she'd been there with him. He'd sensed her approving smile widen with every day he got further away from his old self.

A few lucky times he felt Cassie too, but from her he got the overriding impression of disappointment. One day he'd prove her wrong.

★ ★ ★

Jay's hair ruffled in the hot wind when he stepped onto the tarmac in Lusaka. In the bustle of people it was a relief to spot his name on a board held by a tall, gangly man wearing an old-fashioned safari suit and with the sort of deep tan only acquired after years in the tropics.

'Pierre La Pont,' he introduced himself. 'Great to see you. This way. Our driver's got the car over by the door, I told him to watch it well or he won't get paid. Grab your bags and let's go; it's a long drive to Choma and we won't get there before midnight. Your insides will be shaken to pieces by then, but it's all good, right?'

Jay grunted a reply and the Frenchman chattered away happily as they travelled. Fancy European style hotels, wide streets crowded with people, animals, vendors, dust and noise — everything assaulted Jay's jet-lagged brain. Pierre kept up a constant rundown of everything they were seeing; the culture, traditions, dress, anything he considered Jay might need to know. It would all be forgotten in the morning when the fog cleared from his head.

At one point Jay slept despite the constant bumping over rough roads and pot-holes.

'We've got a flat tire. Out you get!'

Pierre laughed and Jay was unceremoniously hauled from the battered car and dumped to sit by the road until they were done.

He'd meant to be totally cognisant for his first impression of Choma but was only vaguely aware of people shaking his hand, being given tea to drink and finally a chance to sleep. A mosquito net shrouded bed, too short and lumpy, but ready to be crawled into and perfect for sinking into complete unconsciousness.

★ ★ ★

A month later Jay tried to write in his journal, the one he'd promised Mary he'd write for the boys. She'd said it would broaden their horizons. He put down his the pen — he was failing everyone here and he'd once thought himself such a hotshot.

He'd been set to sort out the local AIDs organisation, make their management system more efficient and get them financially stable, but he'd made as much progress as walking through a vat of glue. If he didn't talk to someone soon he'd tear his hair out, so Jay headed across the compound to Pierre's small bungalow and prepared to vent.

'Jay, Jay, Jay . . . ' Pierre shook his head after Jay ranted for a full half hour. 'Do you know how long this continent has suffered, how long it's taken for things to get this bad? Did you think you were going to wave a magic wand in a few short months and make it all well? You're a perfect example of why I'm dubious about these short term assignments. Remember what you were told?'

They'd warned him before leaving London not to expect too much but he'd bounded off the damn plane with the naiveté of a five-year-old on his first day of school before it sinks in that the world doesn't revolve around them.

'We've got to get your focus back on the task you were given. You'll take a day off tomorrow and we'll go to

Victoria Falls. I promise you'll see everything with fresh eyes on Monday.'

Jay hoped he was right or he might as well get on the next plane home.

The next morning the crashing thunder of water filled Jay's senses. He stood on Knife Edge Bridge, soaked by the spray from the falls despite having paid five thousand kwacha for rented rain gear, but making no attempt to move on. He mentally thanked Pierre for leaving him alone — his boss had stayed at the craft village saying he wanted to buy some gifts, but Jay knew a cover story when he heard one. Pierre knew precisely how to get the best from the people he was sent and possessed people skills successful companies would kill for.

Mosioa-Tunya, 'the Smoke that Thunders' was the old tribal description Pierre passed on to him, and it perfectly described the amazing waterfall filling his vision. The dramatic, living sheet of water plummeted over a sheer wall of stone and changed the peaceful Zambezi river into a raging torrent. He'd traveled widely but compared to this experience the glorious beaches in Bali and the ancient Roman Coliseum were tame and ordinary.

Surrounded by the overwhelming noise, Jay felt oddly at peace. *I can do this,* he told himself. *I can make a difference — a small albeit but worthwhile nevertheless.*

Jay started the climb back down the gorge to the Boiling Pot at the base of the falls. The steep trail tugged at his thigh muscles in a good way and he found a vantage point on one of the rocks. For a while he watched a bunch of crazy bungee jumpers falling from the bridge straddling Zambia and Zimbabwe. Jay decided he wasn't that desperate for excitement.

He strolled back to join Pierre in the gift shop and dutifully spent money on locally made crafts to take home. Of course they would all look garish and out of place in cold, gray Ireland but that wasn't the point.

'Ready to go back?' Pierre asked and Jay met the older man's kind eyes. He nodded and the Frenchman smiled.

They didn't talk much on the long drive back to Choma and Jay's mind raced with new ideas to try tomorrow, things he should have seen before but was too blind to recognise. He couldn't wait to get to his room and scribble down his thoughts.

Hours later he dropped the pen and stretched the cramped muscles in his hand. Using the laptop would've been more efficient but there'd been something infinitely more satisfying about filling the lined pages of his writing pad.

Jay rubbed at his brow and the beginning of a dull headache. He stripped down to his boxers and lay on his bed. Slowly his mind drifted into a half-asleep haze and Cassie's face emerged. This time it was no longer etched with disappointment and the trace of a smile turned up the corners of her soft, full lips. For a second he felt her springy, blonde curls under his fingers, but then the feeling was gone. It was torment to reach into the empty air and Jay's body hummed with frustration.

He couldn't imagine going back yet and wouldn't allow himself to think so far ahead. All his concentration must be on doing what he'd been sent here to achieve and the rest would become clear when the time was right. Jay laughed quietly into the darkness. His father had always said, 'Patience, my boy, patience.' He'd never listened before but he'd practice it as his next task.

* * *

Cassie hummed to herself and slipped on the new yellow dress she'd picked up earlier in the week. Normally she tied her hair back to go out but Tony had asked her to leave it loose.

Somehow they'd got into an enjoyable Saturday night date habit. It wasn't supposed to be a real date although the line was beginning to blur. A little hand-holding here and there, the occasional light kiss on the cheek, private jokes that weren't funny to anyone else. She guessed this was closer to the dating 'normal' people did.

'Your boyfriend's here.' Sam laughed without humor.

Cassie barely held back from telling him to shut up. Pete seemed to encourage Sam to make fun of Tony, although he'd stared her down and denied it when challenged.

'Thank you.'

'Not denying it today then?' Sam teased.

'What's the point? You don't take any notice when I do.'

Sam stormed out, slamming the door behind him. Cassie let out the breath she'd held onto.

It never hurt a woman's confidence to be admired and Tony's eyes crinkled into a broad, warm smile when she walked into the living room.

They were joining some friends of his at a new upscale Italian restaurant in Falmouth so tonight Tony wore a suit and tie. It was black linen, creased exactly right, worn with an immaculate white shirt and a startling red silk tie adorned with a gold dragon. There was enough of the actor remaining in him to enjoy playing to an audience and he'd left his hair loose too, a dense foil of shiny blonde against the black of his jacket shoulders.

Sam mocked Tony for being girly but in Cassie's opinion there was nothing feminine about him. And neither of them had mentioned Jay in weeks.

'Have a good evening.' Pete's bland words echoed with the vaguest touch of sarcasm and Cassie noticed him exchange a small smile with Sam.

'Thank you again for staying,' she said politely.

Pete gave a mock salute. 'My pleasure.'

\* \* \*

'You're quiet.' Tony commented as they reached town and she caught the concern in his voice.

'What's your opinion of Pete?'

Tony gave a wry laugh. 'Wow. That's a loaded question. Do you mean as your ex, as Sam's father, or as a man?'

'I don't know. All of the above. You're an actor. Can you tell when someone else is acting?'

He turned into the car park and brought the car to a stop.

'Not always. The first day Pete came into the shop something about him made me feel uneasy and the feeling hasn't gone away. He has a plan and he's not sharing.'

'Do you think he'd hurt Sam?' she asked, although wasn't sure if she wanted an honest answer.

'Hurt Sam? I don't think he'd physically hurt him but I'm not sure about anything else. They talk a lot and he doesn't like being overheard does he? I suppose it's just father son stuff, but remember he survived prison multiple times. I'm pretty sure you learn to act there if you didn't know how before.'

'What can I do?'

Tony shook his head. 'That's another question entirely. You've no proof and Sam will fly off the handle if you hint all might not be as it seems. It's a balancing act. Have you ever been in the circus before?'

The twinkle in his eyes belied the seriousness of the subject.

Cassie gave in and laughed along with him. 'No. There's not been much opportunity for tightrope walking in my life.'

'You might need to do a crash course, then.'

Cassie went quiet for a moment. 'You're right. Let's enjoy our evening and I'll worry about the rest of it tomorrow.'

Tony bent close enough that she smelt his fresh lime cologne, and brushed her cheek with his lips. 'I'm happy to obey your order. Let's go suck spaghetti together!'

232

★ ★ ★

Cassie took another sip of the delicious Sicilian wine and allowed its light fragrance to fill her awareness as she sat back and let the conversation swirl around her, watching Tony without him noticing. He was engrossed in telling his friends about a strange customer they'd had last week, the lady who'd talked to a small green and yellow bird perched on her shoulder.

She smiled inside, loving his exuberance. His friends were all friendly and welcoming and they'd easily accepted her — if she remained a little awkward it was her own doing. All six of them were well-educated and free with their opinions which made her retreat slightly, afraid of not matching up.

Tony's hand rested on hers and gave a reassuring squeeze. She met the concern in his eyes, smiled, and he turned away to concentrate his attention on a joke Holly was telling.

Holly, raven-haired and gorgeous,

233

gave Cassie the only sharp look of the evening when they met. The man with her was obviously only a friend and Cassie noticed the possessive looks she threw in Tony's direction. Cassie mulled over how that made her feel. No red-hot streak of jealousy rose up inside, nothing to compare to the furious possessiveness she'd feel if it was Jay that another woman was eyeing up.

Tony was the dearest friend she had, wonderful company, smart and funny . . . But she wasn't being fair to him. She'd rationalised it away but there was really no excuse. He deserved more than friendship and the occasional kiss on the cheek.

She'd have to be clever; like most men he had to think it was his idea. Cassie took a deep swallow of wine, turned on an amused smile, and joined in the conversation.

A little later, she pulled the old girly trick of going in pairs to the bathroom, and as she stood in front of the mirrors she sighed, 'I wish mine would behave as easily as yours.'

Holly stopped combing her shiny black curls and her dark eyes warily studied Cassie in the mirror.

This wasn't going to be easy. How did she match-make another girl with a man who'd made it plain to everyone in the room he was only interested in her?

'Yours is very striking. You must have been told that before?'

Cassie chose to take Holly's neutral tone as a slight improvement and carried on. 'Trust me you don't want all these curls. All I can do is wash it, leave it to dry naturally and pull my fingers through it. It breaks any comb I try to put near it and brushing it is akin to torture.'

Holly laughed freely. 'I don't know if that's worse than the heated rollers I inflict on mine every morning — and again in the evening if I'm going out. It's as straight as old-fashioned stair rods if I don't do anything. Crazy, isn't it? You've got natural curls and curse them and I go through endless torments to get curls.'

'I bet it'd look lovely straight — it's such a gorgeous color and so glossy.'

'Tony said that too.' Holly's cheeks colored and she glanced away. She grabbed a lipstick from her bag and concentrated on making her full lips a deeper shade of red.

*Careful what you say*, Cassie cautioned herself. 'He's funny isn't he? He says he likes natural women but it's an actor's idea of natural, where it doesn't look as if you've tried too hard, but you have really.' Let that sink in. 'Have you known him long?'

Holly blotted her lips with a tissue, freshened her eye shadow, and wielded a mascara wand over her already impossibly long lashes. 'Yes. All the time he's lived here. We met at the local drama group.'

'Do you act too?'

'Backstage. I do the make-up.' Of course, it should've been obvious. 'And you?' Holly asked with a sharp edge to her voice.

'Only since I started to work in the book shop. We're good friends, enjoy each other's company very much, but that's all.'

Holly's beautifully plucked eyebrows raised at Cassie's assertion. 'Really? It doesn't look that way.' Cassie held her tongue and the other woman filled the silence. 'He can't keep his eyes off you,' she stated sadly.

'He's lonely, Holly, and I'm around a lot. We're very good friends and sometimes it can be misinterpreted.'

Holly pinned Cassie down with a fierce stare.

'This isn't any of my business,' Cassie went on without hesitation, 'but sometimes we don't see the things right in front of our eyes. We get so used to people being around we hold onto the same opinion we formed when we first met.'

A chill ran through her as she realised that was what she'd done to Jay

— always hearing and seeing him as he'd been by the hotel pool in Italy. Maybe he'd changed too? But if she gave him a second chance did she have to give Pete one too? Cassie's hand went to the lingering, dull ache at her temple.

'Are you OK?' Holly asked with concern.

'Yes, I'm fine.' She must seize her chance now. 'Why don't you invite Tony for dinner or to the cinema sometime? But don't tell him I suggested it, of course.'

Holly went very quiet and whispered. 'Are you sure?'

Cassie nodded and held out her hand. 'Positive.'

They shook on it and a weight lifted from her shoulders. Hopefully she'd put right one of the wrongs she'd done.

# 12

Pierre pumped Jay's hand vigorously as he told him, 'Don't forget us. You've done a great job. Officially it's over, but you made promises so you'd better keep them.' He nodded towards the group of people in colorful ceremonial dress gathered outside the office ready for Jay's send-off.

Tears burned the back of Jay's eyes and his heart clenched with a feeling he couldn't give a name to as his glance swept over the people he'd worked closely with the last three months.

He'd got all the new computers up and running with enough people trained to use them. The budget was balanced for the first time and with a solid business plan in place the clinic could treat more people. Jay had helped achieve that for them but he'd got so much more in return.

Beyond the flight home and his debrief in London his only plan was to go to Ireland and reconnect with his family. After that he'd no clue. He'd fundraise for the clinic but sensed it couldn't be his whole life. In a perverse way the easy thing would be to go on another assignment, but he'd promised himself not to do easy anymore.

'Time we were going. You'll be alright you know,' Pierre announced sagely. 'Don't be so hard on yourself.'

Jay scrutinised Pierre's wide, bright blue eyes holding the openness of a young child although they'd seen so much misery over the last twenty years. He possessed the same calm contentment as Jay's father — achieved by being men who'd found their place in life. Jay longed to find his place. He'd edged closer the last few months, but wasn't there yet.

Jay nodded, unable to speak. Bending down he ruffled the tight, soft curls on the heads of the two children clinging to Pierre's legs, then picked up his bags and they all swarmed around him, dancing and singing a traditional local farewell song.

It was then that he gave in to the emotions swamping him, uncaring of the tears running down his face.

Gently Pierre extricated him and they headed towards the Land Rover. His last view of Choma was a multitude of hands waving through a cloud of dust.

* * *

'My God, they've taken my brother and sent a hippie in his place. Mary will have a fit!' Eamon grasped Jay in a tight hug, not letting him go for way past their normal two seconds.

Jay stood back and grinned, showing off his white teeth against the deepest tan he'd ever had. He kept his thick, dark, unkempt hair back out of his eyes with a colorful bandana. It had been a gift from the children in Choma and was green, red, black and orange — the colors of the Zambian flag. One of the older girls printed a matching cotton shirt for him and he wore it proudly even though it was two sizes too big. His worn khaki shorts were the ones he'd worked and often slept in.

Hand-made leather shoes were something from his past and he'd bought today's locally made rope sandals at the market for a few thousand Kwacha, the equivalent of about fifty pence.

His glossy ex-girlfriends would kill themselves laughing.

'Good to see you, too. I'm glad I traveled a few thousand miles for this happy reunion.'

Eamon slapped Jay's back. 'Come on. Let's get some good Irish food into you. You're like a skeleton.'

Jay prodded his brother's slight paunch. 'I'm a healthy skinny, unlike some people I could mention. Not that I'll turn down a plate of Mary's stew and a pint of Guinness.'

'Better than the stuff you've been

eating by the looks of you,' Eamon teased.

Jay tried to imagine his brother eating Nshima, the thick local porridge, and maybe some fried mswa — flying ants. His meat and potatoes brother would be thin too, on that diet.

They drove home in silence, Jay wanting nothing more than to soak in the soft, rain-hazed scenery and lock every inch of it clearly in his mind.

At the house his nephews fought over carrying his suitcases in and Andy, the youngest, gave him funny looks, obviously unsure who this shaggy, oddly dressed man was.

Jay opened up his bags and began to share out the presents he'd brought back. He wasn't sure which Mary would consider worse — the noisy painted drums, the fake ceremonial daggers, or the gruesome masks. The boys landed on all of it with whoops of approval, sharing them out with no help from him and racing away to show off their treasures.

He let them go, abandoned the idea of unpacking and stared longingly out the window.

Day after day in the oppressive heat and dust he'd longed for this view. Deep emerald green grass soaked with heavy misty rain on undulating hills spreading far off into the distance. Neat farm buildings and stone walls contrasted strongly in his mind with tin-roofed shanties and flat, worn-out land.

'Out you go, little brother, get yourself some boots and waterproofs by the back door and we'll see you later.'

Jay met Eamon's steady gaze. 'You sure? I ought to . . . '

'We're family. There aren't any ought-to's. I don't go away much but when I do Mary shoves me out there as soon as I return. It steadies me back down.'

Jay nodded, turning away so his brother wouldn't see the overwhelming sensations flooding through him again. These days his emotions lay barely under the surface and it took so little to set them off.

'The stew will keep,' Eamon said. 'Of course my vultures might have finished it all, but as much as Mary loves you she won't let you starve. She'll get her own back when you have to tell us every detail of your trip. She's lived another life through your emails these last few months. She won't tell you but she's been envious and I've felt guilty because she's never had the chance to go anywhere.'

Jay shook his head slowly. 'She wouldn't change her life for anything and nor would you. I understand a lot more now about choices and consequences. I won't be as reckless with whatever I decide to do next.'

'Does that apply to women too?' Eamon asked quietly stepping over a line the brothers usually avoided.

'Yeah, well, I . . . there's . . . ' Jay flushed, helpless to know how to carry on.

Eamon flashed a mischievous grin. 'I don't believe it. You've cracked at last. Mary said you would eventually.'

'Discussing me, were you?' Jay tried to sound cross but couldn't manage anything more than mild indignation. Nobody else cared enough about him to wonder.

'Of course. We're married; it's what husbands and wives do. So who's the lucky creature?'

'Her name's Cassie Moore. I don't know why I'm bothering to tell you any of this because she's thrown me out several times and told me to grow up or not bother coming back.'

Eamon's raucous laughter filled the room.

'Oh boy, that's typical womanly wiles for you! They know exactly what to do to tame and civilise us and we fall for it every time. You're working out how to get back in her good books aren't you, you sorry creature?'

'Get back in them? I've never been there yet — I may have got close a few times but that's about it. You got any ideas?'

Eamon smirked. 'I never thought this day would come — you asking me for advice on women? How have the mighty fallen!'

Jay threw up his arms in fake disgust. 'If all you can do is crow I'm going for a walk now and you can take a running jump.'

'Sorry, I couldn't resist.' Eamon struggled to appear sorry but failed miserably. 'So go on then, tell us a bit more about your mystery woman.'

Jay hesitated but when he started to speak it all poured out, how they'd met and the long rocky path of their relationship.

'Phew! Don't like a quiet life, do you?' Eamon laughed again.

'Yeah, well, you know me. I promised myself I'd sort myself out before I see her again. It might be too late, but I've got to take the chance.'

'Take your time.' Eamon turned serious. 'If you two have something special she'll wait for you to unwind some here until things are clearer. But you don't need everything laid out in a life plan before you see her again. She'll appreciate you being a bit lost and needing her help. Women like nothing better than sorting men out and setting them straight. Mary did it with me.'

'What do you mean? You two were practically engaged in primary school,' Jay joked.

'It wasn't that simple. You were a lot younger so you didn't realise. I . . . well, I played around a bit at the agricultural college. Mary wasn't impressed to say the least.'

'You sure you want me to hear all this?' Jay couldn't believe his upstanding brother's confession.

Eamon shrugged. 'You won't broadcast it I hope, the rest of the family don't know. Dad found out and told me to be completely honest with Mary. It was the worst advice he ever gave me. I insisted she heard every detail and to say I'd a lot of groveling to do afterwards is a joke. At one point I didn't think we'd make it to the altar but thankfully we did.'

Jay touched Eamon's shoulder. 'Thanks.'

'What for?'

'Making me feel not quite such a moron.'

Eamon smacked him lightly around the side of the head.

'Oh, you're still that. Always will be, baby brother. Now get off out on your walk or Mary will nab you and you'll never escape.'

* * *

'Mum, you haven't planned anything for half-term next week, have you?' Sam's voice buzzed with excitement.

'No, but I could ask for a couple of days off if there's something special you fancy doing.'

Cassie dished up dinner, mentally crossing her fingers that whatever Sam had in mind didn't involve a lot of money.

'There's no need. Dad's offered to take me with him to visit my other grandparents. He's going to Birmingham on Saturday for a couple of days. Can I go, please?'

Over Sam's shoulder Cassie met Pete's bland expression and her stomach flipped. She took out glasses and started to fill them with water, trying to stop her hands from trembling.

'We'll talk about it later. Let's go ahead and eat before your Gran gets irritated at being kept waiting.'

Sam glared at Pete. 'I told you she'd say that. Discussing it later means no, always has done.'

'That's not fair, Sam.' Cassie touched his arm but he jerked out of her grasp.

'I'm sorry, I didn't mean to start an argument.' Pete explained and turned back to Sam. 'Let's eat your Mum's delicious roast beef and afterwards we'll talk. She's a reasonable woman, Sam, give her some credit.'

Why did his reasonable sounding words chill her? Cassie steadied herself and tried to smile.

'Thanks. Sam, go and tell Gran and Grandpa dinner's ready.'

But in spite of her best efforts, dinner was a tense affair.

'You go and sit down in the other room and we'll clear up, won't we, Sam?' Pete said when they'd finished eating.

Cassie felt manipulated but couldn't resist Pete's sheepish grin and the swift way Sam's sullenness was replaced by an agreeable expression. She was given a cup of coffee and the newspaper so she'd give in for a while and enjoy the break. It didn't mean she was going to agree to anything she wasn't comfortable with.

Eventually they came back in and Pete nudged Sam to sit by Cassie on the sofa while he perched on a kitchen chair.

'I'm sorry, Cass, I should've mentioned it to you first, but I got a bit carried away. Mum and Dad have been on at me for a while to bring Sam for a visit. They missed seeing him growing up, but that was all my fault not theirs. They were good parents, you know — my sisters both turned out alright. I was the hard-nosed rebel kid who wouldn't listen.'

Guilt swept over Cassie.

'I'm sorry too, Pete. I should've taken Sam to see them before now. They were kind to me all those years ago and I shouldn't have made them pay for your mistakes.'

His dark eyes bored into her. 'You did what you could. It couldn't have been easy and they did move a long way away. They'd love to meet Sam, so will it be all right for him to come?'

What could she say? Cassie pushed Tony's comments about Pete and her mother's pithy opinion from her mind. Sam deserved this chance.

'All right, as long as you're back no later than Wednesday. Sam's got an art project to finish before school starts.'

'I'm busy at work so I can't take the whole week off.' Pete seized her hands.

'You don't know what this means to me.'

She wanted to pull away from his grasp but it would be too obvious and unkind so she left them there. 'I need to do the ironing if you've finished in the kitchen.'

Pete let go of her but she wondered how long he'd have held on if she hadn't made an excuse to move.

★ ★ ★

'You're a fool, Cassandra. Always have been where that man's concerned.' Her mother shook her head and took another sip of tea.

'Oh Mum, please, that was seventeen years ago. I've grown up since then even if you don't see it. How would you like to have a grandson you'd never seen? Surely you can understand their feelings?'

'Don't pull the old guilt thing on me, young lady. Of course I understand, but who's to say his story is the truth? What

253

if he disappears with Sam?'

Cassie laughed. 'You've been watching too many true crime stories on TV. They're going to Birmingham not China and I've got the address and phone number.

Barbara wagged her finger in warning. 'Fine, don't listen. I'll say one more thing then shut up. If I was you I'd check out the contact details Pete gave you. Can't harm, can it?'

'Yes, it could do a lot of harm. If Pete found out he'd think I don't trust him and I have to trust him for my own sake or I won't be able to let Sam go on Saturday.'

Cassie picked up the book she'd been reading, found her place, and tried to look as if she was concentrating. She was well practiced at ignoring her mother.

⋆ ⋆ ⋆

At work the next morning Cassie knew she needed to plan something to help take her mind off Sam leaving.

'Tony, do you fancy the new James Bond film on Saturday?'

He kept his attention fixed on sorting out a pile of new Cornish guide books. 'I can't, sorry, I'm busy.'

'Oh, alright. How about Sunday instead?' She continued working on the display table in the front of the shop.

Tony turned around and she glanced up but he didn't quite meet her eyes. A flash of color tinged his cheekbones as he walked over to her. He took the book she held in her hand and dropped it onto the table before taking both her hands in his.

'Cassie. I've been trying to tell you something for a couple of weeks but I'm a coward. You'll say I'm stupid.'

She touched a finger to his lips. 'Stop right there. I'd never say that to you. You're my best friend.'

He shrugged. 'Sorry. It's me being . . . oh hell, Cassie, I don't know how to say this.'

'Whatever is it?' She panicked,

imagining all sorts of dreadful possibilities. 'Surely it can't be that bad?'

'I'm a two-timing jerk. Why should that be anything serious?'

'Who're you two-timing?' Cassie was confused.

'You, of course,' he snapped.

'How can you be two-timing me when we're not dating?'

His sharp green eyes pierced into Cassie. 'Weren't we?'

She'd better choose her words carefully. 'I didn't think we were. I thought we were wonderful friends who enjoyed each other's company when it suited us. Was I wrong?'

Tony's shoulders relaxed and the tension strumming through his body into hers eased. 'No, you weren't — but I think I might've been for a while.'

'OK, so now we've established where we stand, what did you want to tell me?'

He let go of her and shoved his hands deep in his pockets. 'I've been seeing someone. Do you remember my friend,

Holly, from the Italian restaurant?'

Cassie suppressed the cheer threatening to erupt and only allowed herself a moderate grin instead. 'Yes. I really liked her. She's gorgeous and obviously liked you a lot.'

Tony really blushed then, grabbed at a pile of books and promptly knocked them over. They both knelt to pick them up and as their eyes met they gave in to helpless laughter.

'We're a silly pair, aren't we?' Cassie chuckled.

'Are you sure you don't mind?' Tony asked almost wistfully.

For the briefest of moments she experienced a touch of regret, not because she loved Tony in that way but for the fact that she hadn't been able to. He'd make some lucky woman a wonderful husband, but it couldn't be her.

'No, I don't. I'm happy for you and I hope everything works out. Holly's a lovely woman and you're my favourite man in the whole world. Well . . . '

'Don't dent my ego by qualifying the statement.' Tony leaned over and softly kissed her cheek, leaving behind a trace of his familiar lime cologne.

'He's back in Ireland you know,' he murmured.

Cassie struggled to keep her expression neutral.

'I might leave his email address lying around sometime I could leave a phone number too, if I was really careless.'

For a second Cassie bit back tears, but then said firmly. 'Don't bother. We're done.' She deliberately busied herself with the display. 'I've got a lot of work to get on with before we leave tonight, so I'd better get busy.'

★　★　★

Surely picking up the phone and calling was a friendly thing to do, considering they hadn't spoken for six months? Jay didn't have to mention his conversation with Tony yesterday and he certainly didn't intend on

258

mentioning Mary's invitation.

Last night his sly sister-in-law had dished up thick vegetable soup with one hand and unasked for advice with the other, and Eamon had suddenly concentrated very hard on eating when she'd casually dropped Cassie's name into the conversation.

'May often has the perfect weather for walking,' Mary had said. 'If your friend Cassie wanted to come we'd be happy to have her here — and her son too if you think he'd enjoy it.'

Jay had almost choked on a piece of carrot and glared at Eamon who remained bent over his food. The best he'd come up with in the way of a reply was a rather lame, 'I'll think about it.'

He should've told Mary to mind her own business but her earnestness touched him. She cared deeply and wanted him to be happy. That was why the phone was in his hand and he'd almost got through dialing the number about a million times.

'Are you ready?' Eamon stuck his

head round the door. 'Colum's waiting for us to get the drinks in, though it's not like turning forty-seven is anything special. You hit the big one next year, don't you, baby brother?'

*Forty. A man should be settled by then,* Jay thought, *established in his life.* He had fifteen months to go and right now he was homeless and jobless. The fact it was by choice didn't improve his mood.

'You go on. I'll be along soon and tell Col I'm not trying to skive out of my round. I've got to make this call.'

'Before you lose your nerve, eh?' Eamon grinned and gave Jay's shoulder a sharp smack. 'Get on with it and grovel. You can never go wrong doing that where women are concerned.'

He left the room, whistling happily and still laughing out loud.

Fat lot of help he was. Jay picked up the phone and sighed.

It rang immediately with not even the delay of an engaged line to help him put it off a few more minutes. The next thing he heard Cassie's voice and he lost the power to speak.

'Is someone there? If you don't say something I'm hanging up.' Her crisp tones startled him back to sense and Jay forced her name out of his tight, dry throat.

'Jay? Is that you?'

The way her voice cracked speaking his name gave him a tiny sliver of hope.

'Yes, it's me. How're you doing?'

For a few minutes they carried on the conversation of two friends simply catching up on their lives, but then she asked what he was planning to do next, giving him no choice but to take the plunge.

'I'm staying here in Ireland a while longer. I'm considering renting a cottage while I make some decisions and might look for temporary work over the summer, maybe as a climbing instructor, something like that.'

Where the hell had that come from?

'You sound better, more content. Did Africa help?'

'Yes, it did. It was amazing. I'd . . . I'd really like to tell you about it sometime.' He held his breath and let the idea hang.

'I'd like it too.' Cassie spoke very softly, her words almost a caress and Jay gathered his courage.

'I don't suppose you'd care to take a holiday in Ireland for a few days? We could do some hillwalking and you could meet my family. You could bring Sam too, if he'd like.'

He could almost hear her mind racing in circles and sent up a swift silent prayer.

'Thanks for the invitation. I'd prefer to come alone. Sam left this morning with Pete, his Dad. They're in Birmingham visiting Pete's family for a few days. Maybe next weekend when they're back Pete would be willing to stay a few nights and keep an eye on Sam and Mum and Dad.'

'Are they getting on well?' Jay caught a brief touch of hesitation before she spoke again.

'Yes. You wouldn't think they'd only just met.'

In his old life Jay made a lot of money picking up nuances in people's voices and behaviour, whether it was in front of him or over the phone, and he sensed Cassie's unease.

'That's a challenge for you.'

A small sigh traveled down the phone line. 'Yes, it is.'

'But it gives you some freedom and that's good?'

Her sexy smile flashed in his mind and Jay's skin heated at the thought of seeing her again — and maybe much more.

'Shall I book you a ticket for next Saturday?'

He wanted to pin her down before she could overthink his offer and come over all sensible.

'Alright if you're sure your family won't mind.'

'Mind? They can't wait to meet you!' He couldn't say another word and she immediately picked up on his disconcerting quiet, thanking him and saying goodbye.

Jay threw the phone on the bed and leapt in the air like a little kid. 'Bring it on!'

He'd get it right this time if it killed him.

★　★　★

Cassie purposely selected her oldest, plainest underwear, as if that'd be a deterrent. In the bag went jeans, a couple of t-shirts, a sweater, waterproof jacket, books and socks. Cassie smiled, remembering their walk on Bodmin Moor. Hiking boots and faded jeans hadn't dampened his libido in the least that day — or hers either. She zipped the bag shut before she could change her mind and repack yet again. In the morning Tony would run her to the station in time for the early train to Exeter and after that it would be a short flight to get her to Dublin before lunchtime.

The journey was the easy part.

One glimpse of Jay's broad smile as he spotted her at the arrival gate and all her good intentions flew out of the window.

'Cassie, darlin', I was so afraid you'd change your mind.'

His strong hands cupped her face and his silvery eyes drew her in, shining brightly in his deeply tanned face. Cassie reached up to touch his hair, a dark silky mass grazing his shoulders, and took in the worn blue jeans, tight black t-shirt and old leather boots.

The smooth persona was gone and the man standing in front of her was Jay stripped to the bone. She struggled to keep her head and heart above water.

'As if I'd waste a plane ticket and the chance to get away from my demanding family for a few days.'

'Is that the only reason you came across the sea to Ireland?' The lilt in his voice was stronger, another clue he'd dropped the shields he'd used so long for protection.

Jay's arms snaked around her waist and he pulled her against him, his hard body reminding her of one of the activities she'd discarded as not on the timetable for the weekend.

'Of course. What else did you think?' Cassie heard the unsteadiness in her voice.

He didn't answer but his eyes spoke words so deep it shook her to the core.

'Let's go. I want to take you home.' Jay grabbed Cassie's bag and her hand, leading her towards the car park.

'What's this? Come down in the world have we?' Cassie grinned as Jay stopped beside an extremely battered Land Rover. She speculated it might have been dark green once but wasn't certain underneath the accumulated dirt of farm life.

'This is Eamon's. I sold the BMW and bought an old Volvo to run around in until I left, but I got rid of it and haven't bothered getting a replacement yet.'

'You've changed.'

Her quiet comment made him turn and stare hard into her soul. 'Is that good or bad?

She chose her words carefully. 'We'll see shall we?'

Jay leaned over and pressed a quick, soft kiss on her mouth. 'Fair enough. Now let's go and meet the five thousand.'

'Oh, goodness, that sounds scary!' Cassie struggled to smile, shaking inside at the idea of being on display.

'It's OK. You'll only have to face Eamon, Mary and the kids to start with. The rest are coming for Sunday lunch. You'll charm them all, don't worry.'

'Certain of that, are you?' she asked shyly.

'To be sure I am, lass.'

His smooth, Irish lilt ran over her skin, soothing the brief surge of apprehension threatening to bubble to the surface.

# 13

Three scrubbed faces examined her so she did the same in return. All peas from the same pod. Thick dark hair plastered wetly to their heads, eyes blue as a summer sky framed with long black lashes, skin deeply tanned from outdoor life, sturdy bodies and the devastating Burton smile.

'Let me see if I've got this right. You're the oldest, Andy?'

The little boy beamed until the other two broke ranks and started to pummel him.

'Stop that now or you know what will happen.' Mary's firm voice silenced the warring children in a matter of seconds.

'I'm sorry. It was my fault for teasing,' Cassie said.

Mary's face softened. 'You've only got one yourself, lass. It's a permanent competition with this lot, morning till night.'

'You have your hands full. I shouldn't have come.' Cassie said with a frown. 'You don't need visitors causing more work.'

Mary's warm, work-roughened hands seized Cassie's and held on tight. 'Any friend of Jay's is welcome and it's a pleasure to have you in our home.' Her eyes crinkled as she gave a girlish giggle. 'Besides, ever since he mentioned you I've been dying of curiousity. If he hadn't invited you I'd have done it myself.'

A rush of heat lit up Cassie's face. She hadn't expected such forthright interest. 'You're not the only one. I've been longing to meet you all too.' Uncertain how much to say she carried on, 'I wasn't sure it would ever happen though.'

'Nor was I, dear,' Mary whispered in her ear.

'Have you two forgotten I'm here?' Jay sighed loudly and folded his arms with a hint of disgust.

'Of course we have.' Mary teased. 'Take Cassie and her bags up to the attic room, show her where the bathroom is then leave her to catch her breath before she joins us for tea.'

'Yes, ma'am. Any other orders?' Jay mocked.

'Behave yourself while you're up there.'

'As if I wouldn't.' Jay tossed back, along with a wicked grin.

Cassie must've been stupid to believe she could resist him for four whole days. Less than an hour in his presence and she was counting the seconds until he touched her again.

Jay led them around the old farm-house, down several long hallways and up two flights of uneven stairs, the wood underfoot rubbed to a soft honeyed color by generations of foot-prints.

'Oh Jay, it's beautiful.' Cassie gazed around the small room. The white walls, dark wood rafters and polished floorboards scattered with dark blue rag rugs charmed her on sight. The brass bed with its blue and white patchwork quilt, probably made by Mary over long winter evenings, was piled high with soft pillows in various shades of yellow.

'You've the best view in the house from here, come and see.' Jay beckoned her across to the window. 'I always wanted this room but Mam used to say guests should have the best we had to offer.' He choked on the words and then went quiet.

Cassie closed the distance between them, wriggled her arms around his body and laid her head against his chest. His firm hand stroked over her hair and gradually his breathing steadied back to normal.

She eased back enough to look up into his dark gaze.

'Why don't you show me where everything is from here?'

His eyes shone with gratitude and she fought against giving in and crying with the simple joy of being with him again.

Jay took her hand and moved it with his own as he pointed out the window. 'The stone walls mark the boundaries of our land. The nearest cottage, the one with all the washing on the line, that's where Colum and his family live.' He reached the far left of the horizon and gripped her hand tightly. 'That's Lugnaquillia, everyone here calls it Lug. Eamon took me up there for the first time when I was ten and he was seventeen.'

'Will you take me?' Cassie held her breath, knowing his choice meant more than just walking together.

'We'll go tomorrow if the weather's alright,' Jay said easily.

'It doesn't have to be good?' she teased and his rumbling laugh took her by surprise.

'No, alright will do. You can wait a long time for good around here.' Jay turned her to face him and trailed a finger lightly down her face, lingering in the hollow at the base of her throat. 'I'd better go before Moralising Mary comes to check on me.'

His wry grin nibbled a gaping hole in Cassie's restraint and his eyes shaded a disturbing molten silver, churning her stomach in pleasant knots.

'Can I have one kiss? After that I promise to leave you unmolested.' He didn't wait for an answer and only touched his lips softly to hers.

The hot, dangerous taste of him surged through her bloodstream until there wasn't a coherent thought in her head.

'You make it hard for a man to leave, you know that, don't you? And I don't use the word hard lightly either.'

Jay struggled to laugh as he pressed himself against her.

'Smooth talker. Go play the part of fun uncle until I come down. If you mind your manners all evening you might get a goodnight kiss,' Cassie said lightly, her body throbbing with unsatisfied desire.

He wound the fingers of one hand through her hair and fiercely pulled her against him with the other. Jay aligned his body with hers in sinuous moves until she gasped.

'Remember I know every creaking floorboard to avoid in the dark,' he growled, his lips moving against the tingling skin of her throat, and with one last devastating kiss he left the room.

★   ★   ★

'Come on around the corner, it's more sheltered.'

Jay gestured to Cassie, hiding a smile as she rested a hand on the rock to steady herself against the sharp wind.

A gentleman would help but he'd offered his hand a couple of times at the beginning of their climb only to receive a disdainful refusal.

He moved over to let her squeeze in next to him, their backs against the rock, knees bent to keep their balance.

'Are you ready for lunch?'

'I'm starved, though I'm sure Mary's packed enough food for a whole army.'

Jay couldn't take his eyes off of Cassie, smiling and glowing with happiness. He loved how she had no qualms about admitting she was hungry. She'd eat heartily and be ready to climb back down, easily keeping up with his longer stride.

He dropped his attention to the backpack, partly to get out the food but also to hide the emotions threatening to overwhelm him. Jay didn't want to frighten her off after he'd waited so long and patiently for this chance.

'Do you want to pour the coffee?' He passed her a thermos and two worn stainless steel mugs. 'We've got beef or cheese sandwiches. How about one of each to start with?'

'Trying to fatten me up, are you? I'll never be stick thin like your usual women if I eat so much,' Cassie joked but Jay instantly seized her hand.

'Do you really think that's what I want, or were you fishing for compliments? You have an amazing figure and I'd prove how keen I am on it if we weren't at the top of a windblown hill bundled up in layers of clothes.'

Her free hand stretched out to rest lovingly against his cheek. 'I'm sorry, Jay. It's just that you've changed on me and I'm just not sure what to make of it.'

Jay's throat closed as he struggled to say the right thing. when Cassie leaned in and nuzzled his stubbly chin and kissed her way up to his lips. Suddenly where they were and the fierce wind and impending rain didn't matter.

He pushed the thermos and back-pack to one side and pulled Cassie close to him. His fingers fumbled to open the fastenings on her waterproof coat, forcing them apart enough to slide his hand between the buttons of her red flannel shirt and up underneath her thermal undershirt.

Finally he touched smooth, hot skin and Jay's body throbbed.

Cassie moaned as they kissed and arched into him, her movement jerking him back to reality.

Jay forced his hands away.

'We can't do this here. I should have more sense. I'll kill us both.' His fingers shook as he refastened her clothes. 'Sorry.'

Her face was flushed and stray curls escaped from her thick plait. 'I should have thought more too but you take all my sense away, Jay Burton. You have done from the first day we met.'

'Mine's been screwed up since then too, you know.'

He risked one light touch of her soft hand. 'This isn't the place for a discussion though, is it? We'll have our lunch, hike back to the farm and politely drink tea with Mary and the boys.'

His dark eyes deepened. 'But tonight I'm coming to you. I can't stay away any longer and I'm pretty sure you don't want me to?' If she said no he didn't think he'd survive.

Cassie shamelessly shook her head, shrugging as if she should know better but had given up.

'We'll make love first because I won't be capable of stringing out a sentence in a room with you and a bed if we don't. Then we'll talk, and I don't mean me telling you only what you want to hear either. After that we'll make love again and I'll go back to my room so we don't scare any small children in the morning.'

Jay laid out his intentions plainly and waited.

Cassie kissed him then pulled away with a lingering smile. 'Get those sandwiches out before I die of hunger.'

'You're a hard woman, Cassandra Moore.' Jay laughed freely and opened up the food.

For a while they contentedly ate the thick sandwiches made with Mary's homemade crusty bread and took in the scenery.

'It's beautiful, Jay. Thanks for bringing me here.'

Her expressive eyes, today as dark a blue as the most precious sapphire, turned his heart to complete mush.

He'd never brought any woman to Lugnaquillia. Today had been a conscious decision and he didn't regret it for a moment.

★   ★   ★

'Two drowned rats. Exactly what I need on my nice, clean floor. Come on, wrap yourselves in these towels and go stand by the oven. When you stop dripping you can go and have a hot bath — separately!'

Mary glared and they did their best not to laugh, but Jay cracked first and then Cassie.

'You're hopeless, Patrick Jay Burton. I only pray this poor woman realises it before she does something she'll regret.' Mary scrutinised Cassie. 'The trouble is I think she already has, so I'm wasting my breath.'

'I'm sorry,' Cassie murmured. 'I was reluctant to start back down because it was so beautiful. Jay tried to warn me the rain was coming but I thought he was just keen to get back for tea.'

Jay grinned. It gave him a kick to hear a woman defending him for a change.

'Oh, get on with the pair of you! You don't get your tea until you're cleaned up and I don't care how hungry the savage is.'

Jay slung an arm around Cassie's shoulder.

'See what she's like to me? Goodness knows why my poor brother married such a witch. You wouldn't treat me that way, would you?' He fixed on his best 'poor Jay' face and Cassie playfully pushed him away.

'I would too, and worse, so be warned. I pity Mary in this house full of unappreciative men.'

Mary shrieked. 'Get off you!'

Eamon sneaked up from behind and squeezed Mary around the waist. 'Come on now, you gorgeous creature. You know we all love you to death and would be lost without you to care for us and civilize us.' He snuggled into her neck and gave her a loud, sloppy kiss. 'Pack them off to get cleaned up. The boys are busy destroying the playroom so I can have you to myself for a few minutes. I can't think what to do with the time, can you?'

'I certainly can! There's a pile of ironing waiting for me and you can clean the floor your dear brother messed up.'

Jay grabbed Cassie's hand and whispered, 'Come on. Can't you see we're not wanted?'

Cassie pulled her towel tighter around herself and stalked off, but at the doorway she stopped and beckoned Jay to follow. He didn't need asking twice.

★   ★   ★

While Cassie luxuriated in a hot bath, Jay stretched out naked on the bed and waited for his body to cool down. No way could he put any clothes on yet. Cassie had taken charge of him and he'd loved every minute of it.

Suddenly there was a loud rap on the door and Eamon called out, 'Pat, get downstairs. There's a phone call for you.'

Jay leapt up, wrapped a towel around his waist and opened up to see his brother's worried face. 'What's wrong? Who is it?'

'It's Cassie's boy, but he's asking for you.'

'I'll throw on my jeans and be right down. Don't let him hang up.' Jay admonished and pushed Eamon away, not even waiting to tell Cassie what had happened.

When she'd finished and saw Jay wasn't there, she'd quickly dressed and gone downstairs, wondering why they were all sitting quietly around the table with the boys nowhere in sight. Everyone stared at her and a detached part of Cassie's brain watched Jay get up and walk across the room.

'I've something to tell you.' He rested his large, sure hands on her shoulders and Cassie was struck dumb, the compassion in Jay's eyes telling her she wouldn't care for what he had to say. 'Sam phoned a few minutes ago.' Jay said quietly and her heart raced out of control.

'He's OK, but . . . '

'But what?'

'He's in hospital with Pete. There was a car crash and Pete's hurt.' Jay sucked in a deep breath and took hold of her trembling hands. 'Come and sit down.' He pulled her onto his lap and she eased into his warm arms. Jay kissed her cheek. 'Drink your tea first, Mary sugared it and I know you don't usually drink it that way but she insists it'll help, and you know we don't disobey her.'

They both failed in an attempt to smile. Cassie forced down a few mouthfuls of the hot, sweet liquid and Jay spoke again.

'Pete and Sam were driving to Birmingham.'

'What the devil were they doing?'

'Give me a chance, Cass.' He stroked her hair and she managed to nod. 'Apparently Pete arranged for a neighbor to look in on your parents and told Sam they were going to Plymouth for the day. But when they got there he carried on towards Bristol. When Sam questioned him Pete spun some story about his mother being ill before he finally admitted he'd planned to go to Birmingham all along. He told Sam he had a new job lined up and they'd be able to live together like they'd talked about.'

'Surely Sam hadn't agreed to do that?' Cassie couldn't keep the hurt from her voice.

Jay sighed. 'No, love. Sam told me Pete mentioned the possibility a couple of times, but he'd said he didn't want to go. Today Pete got real agitated and lost his temper with Sam. He drove faster, took a corner too sharp, skidded on the wet road and hit a tree.'

Cassie only heard his last three words. She screamed and lashed out at

Jay, her hands pounding wildly at his chest. He easily pinned her to him, clasping her to his chest until her body stopped jerking and her breathing slowed.

'You promised Sam was OK, how can he be?' she sobbed.

'He was wearing his seat belt and they hit directly on the driver's side. Sam's bruised and shaken but he sounded as alright as anyone could after a bad wreck.'

Pete came to mind, so proud at reading Sam's last school report and cheering at the last football match when Sam scored the winning goal. Why couldn't he have been content?

'How bad is Pete?' Cassie whispered and caught a pitying glance flash between Mary and Eamon.

'He's still unconscious. He suffered several broken bones and his face is pretty torn up because he went straight through the windscreen.'

Jay's calm, steady words kept her from losing it completely but her eyes flooded with tears she struggled not to shed.

'I have to go.'

'I know, darlin'. Go pack your bag and Eamon will take us both to the airport.'

'But . . . '

'Don't say it, don't even think it. I'll call about flights to Bristol while you pack,' Jay ordered and Cassie leaned closer to give him a brief kiss. She didn't say anymore.

★ ★ ★

'No way. We'll wait for the next flight.' Cassie squirmed under Jay's fierce glare.

'Don't be ridiculous. Sam needs you and it's only money.'

'But it's ridiculously expen — '

Jay turned to the short, balding man behind the desk and nodded agreement. He seized Cassie's hand and steered her across to the corporate lounge.

'Sit there. I'll get us some coffee.'

He pushed her down onto the nearest seat.

Cassie wanted to storm out and tell him she wasn't going to be ordered around, but the anger bubbling up inside her slowed to a simmer.

He was doing this from love. It might not be tactful, it might not be politically correct, but it was Jay's way to assess a situation, make a decision and implement it. The next available regular flight wasn't until the morning so he'd agreed to charter a private corporate jet and it was lined up to take off within the hour. There'd be a car waiting at Exeter to take them straight to the hospital. He'd even spoken to the doctor in charge of the critical care unit, got an update on Pete and confirmed Sam's minor injuries.

Jay returned and set two cups of steaming coffee down on the table in front of her.

As he sat down beside her his arm snaked around her shoulder and his strong fingers rubbed at a tense, sore spot.

'Sorry, darlin', but I can't let you suffer all night when it's not necessary. This is something I can do so let me, please.'

Cassie gave in, seeing the clear worry in his suspiciously shiny eyes. How could she not love this man?

Her head dropped to Jay's chest and she laid it against his heart. 'No, I'm the one who should be sorry. Thanks for everything. It doesn't really say what I feel but if I'm too honest I'll collapse in a blubbering mess and I daren't do that yet.'

He tipped up her chin to look at him, treating her to one of his wry smiles. 'When you're ready to blubber, please feel free. I have excellent shoulders for soaking up tears.'

Cassie allowed a tiny smile to escape. He was hard to resist — no, make that impossible. Her fingers walked across his shirt. 'You actually have excellent shoulders for all sorts of things but we won't discuss that now.'

A rush of color tinged his face and her smile widened.

'Drink your coffee.'

His voice turned husky and Cassie relished the fact she could affect him so strongly almost at will. She obediently sipped the lukewarm liquid as they waited together.

\* \* \*

'You want Teign Ward, mate, second floor.'

Cassie heard Jay thank the taxi driver as she ran towards the door. The seemingly endless ride up in the lift hollowed out her stomach and she burst through the doors as soon as they opened. She looked around for the waiting room and, spotting Sam through the glass doors, Cassie raced in to him.

'Mum . . . ' Sam burst into tears and flung himself into her open arms.

'Oh, love, it's alright.'

Sam winced as she gave him a brief, hard hug and she let go.

'Sorry, did I hurt you?'

'Yeah, a bit, but it's OK. It's bruises from where the seat belt got me.'

His dark eyes flooded with pain and Cassie stood back to examine him properly. His hands were covered in small cuts and scratches and so was his face.

'That's from the glass. Dad went through the windscreen.' Sam's voice cracked but he struggled on. 'Wasn't wearing his belt, was he. It was awful. There was blood everywhere. All over me. When they got me here . . .'

Cassie gently stroked a patch of unmarked skin on the side of his face, needing the reassurance of knowing he was alive.

'Hey, Sam. What is it with us and hospitals? You didn't have to do this to get me back to England, I was coming anyway,' Jay exclaimed as he casually strolled into the room.

Cassie watched her son straighten up

and pull back together, making her love Jay even more.

'You look like a man in need of food and I am too. How about we go and get something. Your mother can call my mobile if she needs us.'

Cassie almost protested but a flash of relief lightened Sam's face and she recognised Jay was right again. She forced out a smile, sat down and picked up an old magazine as she watched them leave together.

Barely twenty minutes later a young man in a white coat came into the room.

'Cassie Moore? I'm Doctor Morgan. I need to talk to you about Pete Wilson.'

She met the young man's dark serious eyes, full of compassion, and her stomach clenched.

# 14

'More tea?' Jay poured them both another mug of strong tea. Sam had already demolished a plate full of bacon, eggs, sausages, baked beans and four slices of toast in about ten minutes flat.

'I thought you said you were hungry? You haven't had anything.' Sam glowered.

'I lied. I didn't think you'd agree to come if I said it was for your sake.' Jay received another glare.

'Yeah, well, you're good at that. Why was Mum stupid enough to go running off to Ireland when you clicked your fingers?' Sam asked with a defiant sneer.

He'd planned a conversation about Pete but the boy wasn't going to wait until later and he couldn't blame him.

'Sam, I won't give you a bunch of

bull. I didn't treat your mother the way I should have and you're right to call me out. I was stupid.'

He took a deep breath and told Sam all about his family.

'I needed to strike out on my own. I'm not cut out to be a farmer and they realised it too. The trouble was, I went astray and when I met your mother I was beginning to get dissatisfied, but didn't know why. It's taken me a while to work it all out and she ended up getting hurt by some of my actions.'

Sam shook his head in disbelief. 'But you're old. You're supposed to know what you want. Hell, I'm supposed to know, at least that's what they tell us in school. What's your problem?'

Jay winced and tried to be honest. 'I was a slow learner. My mother died unexpectedly recently and it shook me up. She'd always known I wasn't happy but I wouldn't let her help.

'But I couldn't carry on the way I'd been doing. Something had to change. Your mum and I almost reached a good point but I still had too many other things to sort out for it to work. That's why I left. Africa made me see what was really worthwhile in life and what wasn't.'

By now he was talking as much to himself as Sam.

'I was desperate to give it another try with Cassie and I asked her to come and visit with no expectations and no promises. She took a chance on me, Sam, and I'm lucky, very lucky. The difference is I realise that now.'

Jay steeled himself for Sam's next verbal barb, but all he said was, 'So what's next?'

*Why don't you just pin me down and pummel me kid, get it over with?* Jay half-smiled, remembering. 'We were getting to that when you called this morning.'

The anger left Sam's face, replaced in an instant by fear and memory. His head sunk into his hands and a tight sob choked from his throat.

*Take a chance,* Jay thought and

moved closer to slide an arm around Sam's shoulder. The boy's head pushed into Jay's chest and wracking tears racked through his body. Jay murmured quiet soothing words into Sam's silky dark hair, so unlike his mother's and wondered if he took after Pete.

'The doctor said you were very brave when they brought you both in. Seeing someone you love in pain and you can't do anything to help is hard.'

'The noise of the crash. It was horrible. No-one tells you it's that loud,' Sam muttered, his voice suffused with horror. He pushed Jay away and jerked up to standing. 'We'd been arguing and that's why we crashed. It's all my fault! If I'd agreed with him it would never have happened.'

Jay stood as well and rested his hands lightly on Sam's upper arms. 'It's not your fault. Your father's a grown man. He made the choice he did knowing it wasn't what you wanted now he's paying an awful price. But that's not your fault and you can't always protect people from themselves.'

'But he's my dad and he could die and I never told him I loved him!' Sam yelled and hot, angry tears dripped down his face.

Tears shimmered in Jay's eyes too and he didn't bother to brush them away. The boy had just said the very thing he'd never been able to put into words himself.

It nearly finished him off after losing his mother — the fact that he hadn't said those words in years.

'He knows, Sam, I promise you he knows.'

He wasn't lying because he didn't need to. His mother was always sure of his love because some things just didn't have to be spoken out loud.

'He sees it every time you smile when he comes to see you and when you give him a quick hug after he praises you for doing well in school. He knew it the first time you called him Dad instead of Pete.'

'You sure?' Sam pleaded in a whisper

and Jay nodded.

'You had your phone turned off.' Cassie's accusing words interrupted the moment and Jay and Sam slowly moved apart.

'I'm sorry. Did you try to ring?' Stupid. Of course she'd tried or she wouldn't know the phone was off. Jay registered Cassie's faint smile and crossed his fingers.

'There's some good news. Why don't you both sit down?'

Jay slipped a hand through Sam's elbow and steered him to the nearest chair. The boy's skin was whiter than chalk.

Cassie perched on a seat the other side of Sam.

'Pete's come round. He's very weak but hopefully he'll be stable enough in the morning for an operation to reset a couple of bones in his leg and he'll need plastic surgery on his face later, too, but he's going to be alright.'

'Can I see him?' The words scraped from Sam's throat.

'Yes, but not for long.'

Cassie stood and headed back towards the door.

Sam jumped up and then turned back, his dark eyes fixed on Jay. 'Come with us, please?'

'Cassie?' Jay needed to be sure she wanted him too.

Gratitude flooded her face and he'd never loved her more. Jay wrapped one arm securely around Cassie and the other around Sam. 'We'll go together.'

\* \* \*

Cassie held back as Sam rushed over to his father's bedside. Pete's eyes were the only thing visible in his heavily bandaged face and as they fixed on her she read his sorrow as clearly as if he'd shouted it from the rooftops.

The last vestiges of anger and resentment seeped away and she realised how fortunate she was and how little life had left him with.

'I'm sorry,' Pete croaked, struggling

to raise himself up and grasping for Sam's hand.

'It's alright. I'm fine,' Sam said with a bravery that brought tears to Cassie's eyes. 'You're going to be OK, Dad, but you won't be able to play football again for a while.'

'Wasn't that good anyway,' Pete forced out the words and fell back against the pillow.

'You're exhausted. We'll leave you to rest and be back in the morning,' Cassie murmured.

'I'm staying,' Sam declared and folded his arms, giving her what he intended as a menacing glare.

Laughter bubbled up inside Cassie but she kept a straight face. 'Alright.' She fumbled in her bag, pulling out some money. 'The cafeteria should still be open, get yourself something to eat and make sure you take a nap later.'

'He'll be fine, won't you, Sam?' Jay said quietly and she got the hint to back off.

'Yeah, thanks, mate.' Sam nodded

and flopped down in a chair by his father.

'There's the name and number of the hotel where we're staying. Call if you need anything — and I mean anything. Right, Sam?' Jay insisted, passing over a slip of paper.

Hotel? When did he arrange that? Cassie gave up and slipped her hand back into his.

'Behave yourselves,' she said in a light-hearted warning and she and Jay left, together again.

\* \* \*

Jay closed the bedroom door and joined Cassie.

'Wasn't this a good idea of mine?'

'It certainly was, you sneaky man,' Cassie sighed as his fingers massaged her tense shoulders, easing out the knots.

'You must be exhausted and starving. Shall I order something from room service?' His hands slid down around her waist and he pulled her into his strong warmth.

'I wouldn't mind a cup of tea, although I expect you could do with something more?'

Jay flashed a quick grin but didn't say a word.

'It's not quite how we expected the day to turn out, is it?' Cassie said with a rueful smile.

'No, but we've still got time, haven't we?'

She heard the catch in his breath and replied with complete truth. 'We've got all the time in the world.'

Relief openly swept over his handsome face. 'That's all I needed to hear.'

Cassie ran her hands up his spine. 'Why don't we forget the tea and go to bed?'

The instant flare in his silvery eyes sent desire flooding through every cell of her body and the tiredness and pain of the day faded away.

'If you insist.'

'I do,' Cassie said, took his hand and

led him to the bed.

They undressed in silence and Jay held out a hand to help her into bed, where he wrapped her in his arms and whispered against her skin, 'We can go straight to sleep if you're tired.'

Cassie slipped her hand down between them and caressed him, loving the way he instantly sprang to life in her fingers.

He groaned and moved against her. 'I get the hint.'

'Make love to me, Jay. Let's end this day right.'

Cassie gasped as he flipped her over, straddling her with his hot, demanding body and sending her into a spiral of uncontrollable desire.

'I'm going to take you slow and tortuous until you plead for more.' His dark words made her shiver and he instantly seized her mouth, sweeping her with his tongue until she drowned in the hot taste of him.

'Wait just a second.' He leaned back on his heels and grabbed a foil packet from the table, but she stayed his hand.

'I don't want anything between us anymore,' Cassie said with calm certainty.

Jay smiled teasingly down at her, eased her thighs wider with his legs and settled into place as he stroked her with his finger, giving a satisfied smile at her obvious arousal.

Jay slid into her slowly, inch by inch, ignoring her pleas for him to hurry. Cassie grabbed around his neck, undulating her hips and urging him on but every time she did he'd withdraw before starting his torture again. The muscles corded in his neck and shoulders as he fought for control and the next time he entered her, Cassie thrust her hips purposefully up, forcing him deep into her.

Jay nipped at her neck until she moaned, making him rear up and plunged back into her, hard and deep. Cassie wrapped her legs around his hips and matched his brutal pace.

She'd never known him completely lose it before but with his eyes screwed shut he punished her with his body and she took all he could give and still craved more. Her body tightened around him and she thundered into her climax, pressing her mouth into his so he'd capture her cry of pleasure. His hands gripped her shoulders and he pulled nearly all the way out before plunging one last time and exploding with his own release.

They grasped each other in desperation as the last aftershocks shook their bodies, Jay's searing hot body slicked against hers and Cassie gasped for breath.

'I can't move, and it's all your fault so don't complain.'

'Wouldn't dare,' she murmured. 'If that's your idea of slow I'm not sure I'll ever be able to handle fast.'

Jay grabbed handfuls of her hair, pulling her to him for another kiss.

'You take every plan I have and turn it upside down. You have done since the day we met and it's why I love you.'

He put a finger to her lips before she could reply.

'Not tonight.' Jay rolled back over onto the bed. 'Time to sleep. We'll talk when I get you back to Ireland.'

She didn't argue.

*  *  *

Cassie peeked out through the bedroom curtains watching Sam trudge across the muddy farm yard to the milking shed.

It was five o'clock in the morning and he was up for the fifth day in a row to help Eamon. Thank goodness she'd given in to Jay's suggestion for Sam to blow off the last week of school and start fresh in January.

Pete was doing well recuperating with his parents and she'd promised Sam he could visit Birmingham in the New Year.

She'd erected all sorts of obstacles, only for Jay to tear them down like a wall made of paper. Her parents were happily being looked after by a friendly caregiver Jay had tracked down and when she'd said she couldn't leave Tony in the lurch at his busiest time of the year he'd found a couple of Sam's student friends to fill in for her.

The last argument she'd tried was that Mary didn't need the extra work of feeding three more people over Christmas, which made Jay roar with laughter.

'You don't know Mary very well, do you? She thrives on it! The more people to nurture the happier the lass is. Anyway, you can help around the house and with the boys and Sam and I will give Eamon a hand.'

The first day Sam had sat in a corner, glared at anyone who spoke, and refused to move from the fire but Andy had broken through his wariness. The sweet five-year-old had poked Sam in the arm and thrust a football at him.

'Uncle Pat says you can kick a ball really far. Will and Seamus are at some stupid birthday party and I'm too small to go. You gonna come play with me?'

A tiny smile tugged at Sam's stern

mouth. 'I guess I can. Is the field muddy?'

Andy nodded, his eyes big with worry, obviously afraid it would put a stop to the idea.

'Good. That's the only way to play.'

Cassie had to clamp down tears as Sam had taken the small boy's hand and led him outside. They'd returned after dark, filthy and starving, and from then on Sam was a different boy.

A happy sigh escaped Cassie's lips.

'He's going to be fine.'

Jay's kind voice brought her back to the moment.

'Forget him for a few minutes because I have a problem that needs solving. For some reason there's not a warm woman in my bed. Come here, you.'

He smacked the bed with his hand and grinned broadly.

'Who do you think you're speaking to?' Cassie tried to sound cross. 'And to think I believed you were a smooth-talking charmer when we met. You were always beautifully dressed and had your flashy car and expensive penthouse. Now look at you.'

She threw him a fake-scathing glance. 'Hair down to your shoulders, you haven't shaved in days, you're mooching off your brother's family and happily unemployed. I can't imagine what I'm doing here with you.'

He leered; it was the only way to describe the sexy, possessive way he dragged his dark eyes down over her body.

'Come here and I'll remind you. This is my first lie-in since we arrived and I don't intend on wasting it.'

'I'm not supposed to be in here with you. Mary will skin us alive if the boys see us coming out from the same room.'

'Ah, darlin' girl. Mary's got a heart of gold. She wouldn't deprive a couple in love of a little pleasure now, would she?'

'A little pleasure? Now that doesn't sound very enticing. I was hoping it would be a big pleasure if I'm risking your sister-in-law's wrath over it.'

Jay flung back the bedcovers.

'Well, what do you think?' He gestured at his obvious arousal with a huge smile and his stifled laughter threatened to explode.

'You're a wicked man, Jay Burton.'

'Yeah, I know. Come here and I'll prove it.'

* * *

An hour later, Cassie languidly ran her hand over Jay's chest, up against his heartbeat. He stopped her hand with his own and gave a wistful smile.

'If you carry on I won't be responsible for what happens. I promise it won't involve talking.'

'Should I put my nightdress back on then?'

'Don't spoil all the fun. I can be restrained when I need to be.' Jay protested.

'Right. With handcuffs?'

'We haven't tried that yet, have we?'

His eyes danced.

'That wasn't an invitation.' Cassie smacked him gently around the head but spoiled the effect by giggling.

Jay played with one of her curls. 'This'll give my hands something quasi-respectable to do while we talk. I want to throw some ideas at you and see what you think.'

'Alright.'

He wasn't hard to read. She'd seen through the surface of him the moment they met, past the handsome Casanova to the lost, good-hearted boy hidden inside.

'I'm not going back to the City, I can't live that life again. But I can't stay here either. You know me, I need a challenge and meeting Sam gave me ideas. I find I empathise with kids his age and can get through to them. There are lots of schemes out there for disadvantaged teenagers. They need to realise they have a place in the world and have responsibilities outside of themselves. I'm thinking of a mixture of education and community work, here and abroad.'

Cassie nodded. 'But where do you even start?'

He gave her a thoughtful look.

'This may sound crazy but I think Pete could be a huge help. He's been about as low as it's possible for a man to get and pulled himself back up. I know he had a glitch there with Sam but he regrets it bitterly and he's determined to make amends. It could give him a chance he might not get otherwise.'

Cassie pressed a gentle kiss on Jay's cheek.

'You're a good man, Jay Burton. That's a wonderful idea. What's your first move?'

'I have to get cleaned up and back in a suit because nobody's going to listen otherwise. I'm good at fundraising and need to get some influential people on board.'

Cassie suddenly bit her lip. Was he leaving again?

As if he had read her mind, Jay

wrapped his hands around hers. 'I need you with me on this. A partnership. A life together.'

Her heart thumped wildly and she could barely force the words from her mouth. 'What exactly are you asking?'

Cassie was too afraid to spell it out in case she was wrong.

'You can't wait, can you? I had it all planned. New Year's Eve, champagne, and a rock you wouldn't be able to say no to. Now you're making me ask you unshaven and naked in bed, and — oh, to hell with it!'

Jay sprung from the bed and dropped to one knee, pulled her nearer and cradled her hands.

'Cassandra Moore, I love you more than life itself. Please, will you marry me? We'll share our families and make them ours together, you and me.'

Cassie stared into his bright, shining eyes, and knew that her own were filled with love and tears.

'Yes, yes! A thousand times, yes!'

A huge grin spread over Jay's

irresistible face and she burned to touch him, running her fingers over tanned skin and stubble.

After a few precious moments where no words were needed she whispered cheekily in his ear, 'So where's the rock then?'

Jay laughed heartily. 'If you'll let me go, you temptress, I'll go and get it.'

She giggled and slid a hand down his chest, playing with the dark curls. 'Not sure I can.'

Jay threw himself back to lie on the floor, arms and legs flung apart in surrender. 'OK, I give in. I'm yours to do whatever you want with.'

'You are *so* easy.'

'Prove it.'

He tossed her another wicked look. The one that wrapped her from her head to her toes with absolute lust.

★ ★ ★

Much later Cassie turned her hand to catch the light and admired her reward

— a stunning two carat square cut diamond set in gleaming Irish gold.

Beside her Jay smirked. 'Don't like it much do you? And you said I was easy.'

'I'd have been equally happy with a cheap ring with a fake diamond,' she insisted in a haughty tone.

'Thank heavens. I'll return it and get the money back, then,' he chuckled and playfully slapped her thigh.

Cassie shoved her ring finger under the pillow and glared possessively. 'You try to take it away and I'll injure your manhood permanently.'

Jay's eyes swept down over his body. 'I think you already have, you insatiable creature.'

But just as they began to entwine their limbs again, there was a loud knock on the door.

'Breakfast time, you two.' Eamon's booming voice came through the locked door. 'Mary's not happy, she had to shoo the boys out so they didn't hear the two of you at it like rabbits. I wouldn't like to be in your shoes for all the tea in China.'

Cassie blushed all over while Jay only laughed.

'Sorry, big Eamon. We'll be down soon and trust me when we tell Mary our news she'll forget all about being mad.'

'It'd better be good,' he warned.

Jay stroked his hands down Cassie's spine and it took all her self-control not to moan in pleasure.

'It is, believe me. It's very good.'

# 15

Cassie screwed up her face, staring into the sun while Jay shifted the sign until it was finally straight. She'd had him up and down the ladder about fifty times so far this morning and judging by his sigh even Jay's patience was wearing thin.

The Burton-Wilson Youth Exchange Center.

When she told him it was too grand a title for the refurbished factory on the outskirts of Truro he said they had to be positive. It was a beginning and not bad going for just six months, although it had been hard work.

'Perfect.' Cassie beamed at him.

'Yes, I know I am.' Jay leapt down and pulled her into his arms. 'Remember that in future, Mrs Burton.'

God, that sounded so good to her ears. Six months on and he still got a kick from calling her his wife. Their quiet New Year's Day wedding was the best idea he'd ever had.

'Did you get your passport in the post this morning?'

Cassie nodded nervously.

'It'll be fine.' He gave her a tight squeeze. 'Pierre's all set to show us around and help plan what's needed.'

Zambia. Cassie had never been out of the country apart from a couple of weekend ferry trips to France. The idea of going scared and exhilarated her equally. Jay had spent hours sharing his experiences there but she was smart enough to know it would be hard.

He wanted her to understand the heart of what they were doing — getting young people out of their comfort zones. It would do more for the teenagers they wanted to help than anything and, combined with the educational courses they had to sign up for, it would open their eyes.

Of course it wouldn't work for all of them and they'd lose some back to the streets and dead-end jobs.

'Where's Tony?' she asked.

'He's on his way. Just picking up his new car.'

Cassie laughed. 'As per instructions?'

'I might've mentioned the managing director of the new centre needed reliable transport which wasn't going to break down on the way to an important meeting. I've promised to get him over to Zambia next year while Pete runs this place for a few months. He needs to really immerse himself there before I send him out fundraising — the rich women won't be able to resist Tony.'

'You're a devious man. He's loving the chance to be involved in this, you know.'

Jay nuzzled her neck and lowered his voice. 'Do you know what he asked me last night?'

Cassie's brain went into overdrive trying to answer the question while not turning to mush under Jay's continued assault on her senses.

'He asked me to be his best man.'

His eyes sparkled.

Cassie pushed him off her and pummeled his chest. 'You horrible man! You mean he's asked Holly to marry him and you kept it a secret all night?'

'Only because you're so much fun to tease. You'll get your revenge later, don't worry,' he said with certainty.

'Damn right I will. I believe I'll sleep in the spare room.'

Jay's hands slid down to her bottom and cupped her to him.

'Behave yourself. We're in public,' she protested feebly.

'It's legal now if you've forgotten, wife.'

'God, don't you two ever stop? I thought once people were married they lost interest in that sort of thing.' Sam jumped off his bicycle, laughing.

He came over to stand by them and suddenly went quiet, his attention fixed on the new sign. 'Dad will love it.' His voice cracked and Cassie squeezed his arm.

'Pete rang this morning and the

doctor cleared him to move back down here next Wednesday. He'll start work here soon as he's settled,' she assured him.

'He's proud of you, Sam. You've helped us a ton getting this ready and to know you're planning to go to university and then work with us here, he's really impressed. We are too.' Jay was the one choked up now.

'Yeah, well . . . ' Sam dropped his head briefly then glanced back up. He fixed his gaze on them both and a flash of color slipped across his face. 'I want to ask you something.'

'What?' Cassie asked, a sliver of worry snaking through her.

'Can Sarah come over for tea tomorrow?'

'Who's Sarah?'

Sam's face turned deep pink with embarrassment.

'She's a friend but I'd like her to be more, maybe . . . We met at school but she wouldn't talk to me until recently.'

Cassie's heart ached. She guessed he

was trying to say this was a nice girl who wouldn't have anything to do with him before. Once you got a bad reputation it was hard to overcome.

'Of course, she'll be very welcome. Any idea what she likes?'

Sam shuffled from one foot to the other. 'Could you make that chicken curry you do sometimes? She likes spicy food. Her father used to work for an oil company and they lived in India for a while.'

'Of course. I'll fix some plain chicken for Gran and Grandpa or poor Sarah will have to listen to them complain all evening.'

Sam stepped closer and bent to kiss her cheek.

'Thanks. You're the best. See you later.'

He leapt back on his bike and rode away with his mobile phone already open and a big smile on his face.

'You got the whole generation range of problems with me, didn't you?' Cassie grinned at Jay.

'Not quite. We've got the elderly parent thing going on and teenage angst but we're missing the small child troubles . . . What do you think about correcting that?'

Cassie blinked under Jay's fixed gaze, unsure if she was understanding him right. 'Do you mean what I think you mean?'

'Tell me what you think and I'll tell you if you're right,' Jay teased with a grin.

She was pretty certain she knew but they hadn't ever discussed the subject. She supposed they should have done before the wedding but it'd been so fast her head never had a chance for a moment's sense.

'Are you saying you want us to have a baby?'

Jay took her face in his hands, smoothing the flush from her cheeks with his kisses. 'I can't imagine anything more wonderful, can you?'

All she could do was nod as tears trickled from her eyes.

'I'll take that as a yes.'

'But it might not happen.' Cassie's face clouded over.

'No, but imagine the fun we'll have trying,' he said playfully.

'You are one wicked man.'

Jay nipped lightly at her neck. 'And haven't you loved it from the moment we met?'

The deep kiss she responded with was Cassie's only answer.

He was right. Again.

## THE END

We do hope that you have enjoyed reading this large print book.

Did you know that all of our titles are available for purchase?

We publish a wide range of high quality large print books including:
**Romances, Mysteries, Classics**
**General Fiction**
**Non Fiction and Westerns**

Special interest titles available in large print are:
**The Little Oxford Dictionary**
**Music Book, Song Book**
**Hymn Book, Service Book**

Also available from us courtesy of Oxford University Press:
**Young Readers' Dictionary**
**(large print edition)**
**Young Readers' Thesaurus**
**(large print edition)**

For further information or a free brochure, please contact us at:
**Ulverscroft Large Print Books Ltd.,**
**The Green, Bradgate Road, Anstey,**
**Leicester, LE7 7FU, England.**
**Tel:** (00 44) 0116 236 4325
**Fax:** (00 44) 0116 234 0205

*Other titles in the*
*Linford Romance Library:*

## SEEK NEW HORIZONS

### Teresa Ashby

Sister Dominique, already having serious doubts about her calling, is sent on a mercy mission to South America after a devastating earthquake. There, she meets Dr Steve Daniels, and feelings she had never expected to experience again are stirred up. As she is thrown into caring for a relentless stream of casualties, her thoughts are in turmoil. How will she cope in the outside world if she leaves the sisterhood? And dare she allow herself to fall in love again?

# HOUSE OF FEAR

## Phyllis Mallett

Jill's twenty-first birthday is more than just a milestone — it marks the day her life changes forever . . . A letter arrives on the morning of her birthday; an invitation to travel to Crag House on the remote Scottish island of Inver to stay with the grandfather whose existence she had been completely unaware of. Whilst there, she meets her cousins, Owen and George, and handsome neighbour Robert Cameron. But her visit has involved her in a web of deceit that may threaten her life . . .

# SUSPICIOUS HEART

## Susan Udy

When Erin discovers that her mother's home and livelihood is under threat from the disturbingly handsome Sebastian, she knows she has to fight his plans every step of the way. However, she quickly realises Sebastian is equally determined to win, and he apparently has the backing of the entire village. When a campaign of intimidation is begun against Erin and her mother, it doesn't take her long to work out that it can only be Sebastian behind it . . .

# THE RUNAWAYS

## Patricia Robins

When Judith and Rocky elope to Gretna Green they sincerely believe marriage will solve all their problems. But the elopement proves to be the beginning of an entirely new set of difficulties ... Rocky begins to wonder if his parents were right — is he even in love? Were they too young after all? And in the background Gavin, Judith's boss, watches her disillusionment with a concern which is growing into something more ...

# ANGEL'S TEARS

## Teresa Ashby

Born in the same year that the Titanic sank, seventeen-year-old Cassandra Grant has the world at her feet. But tragedy strikes her family and Cassie has to grow up fast. She falls in love with Dr Michael Ryan — but then discovers he is about to be engaged to be married. Cassie leaves town to begin training as a midwife and tries to forget Michael, but tragedy strikes again and she has to return home where there are more surprises in store . . .

# DEADLY INHERITANCE

## Phyllis Mallett

1927: Sarah Morton is looking forward to starting her new job as a tutor with a wealthy Yorkshire family, but she is taken aback when her young charge, Justin Howard, claims that someone wants him dead — and his great-grandfather seems to believe the same. Could greed be a motivating factor in the attempts to see off the young heir? And is Justin's handsome Uncle Adam really to be trusted?